ALFRED BESTER

STARMONT READER'S GUIDE 6
CAROLYN WENDELL
Series Editor: Roger C. Schlobin

Starmont House ■ P.O. Box 851 ■ Mercer Island, Washington 98040

PS
3552
E796
Z93
1980

For—

RSFFA—for help and harassment;
in short, for being friends.

Library of Congress Cataloging in Publication Data

Wendell, Carolyn.
  Alfred Bester.

  (Starmont reader's guides to contemporary science fiction and fantasy authors ; 6)
  Bibliography: p.
  Includes index.
  1. Bester, Alfred—Criticism and interpretation.
I. Title. II. Series.
PS3552.E796Z93   813'.54   80-19655
ISBN 0-916732-08-8

Cover by Stephen E. Fabian, Sr. and Jr.

Typesetting by Pendragon Graphics

CAROLYN WENDELL is Assistant Professor of English at Monroe Community College in Rochester, New York. She has been an addicted reader of science fiction since childhood and has published articles on women in science fiction and the teaching of science fiction.

CONTENTS

ABBREVIATIONS

Because of the variety of editions in and out of print, citation is made whenever possible simply to the book referred to or to the chapter within the book; this is done parenthetically within the text. Four abbreviations of Bester's major volumes are used:

TDM   *The Demolished Man*
TSMD *The Stars My Destination*
TCC   *The Computer Connection*
STL   *Starlight: The Great Short Fiction of Alfred Bester*

I.

CHRONOLOGY OF LIFE AND WORKS

1913   Born in Manhattan December 18; son of James J. and Belle Silverman Bester.

1935   A.B. from the University of Pennsylvania.
        Began law school at Columbia University.

1936   Married Rolly Goulko.

1939   "The Broken Axiom," Bester's first science fiction story, which won first prize in a contest sponsored by *Thrilling Wonder* (April).
        "No Help Wanted" (story, *Thrilling Wonder*, July).

1940   "Guinea Pig, Ph. D." (story, *Startling Stories*, March).
        "Voyage to Nowhere" (story, *Thrilling Wonder*, July).

1941   "The Mad Molecule" (story, *Thrilling Wonder*, January).
        "The Pet Nebula" (story, *Astonishing*, February).
        "Slaves of the Life Ray" (story, *Thrilling Wonder*, February).
        "The Probable Man" (novelette, *Astounding*, July).
        "Adam and No Eve" (story, *Astounding*, September).
        "The Biped, Reegan" (story, *Super Science Stories*, November).

1942   Began writing for comic books.
        "Life for Sale" (novelette, *Amazing*, January).
        "The Push of a Finger" (novelette, *Astounding*, May).
        "The Unseen Blushers" (story, *Astonishing*, June).
        "Hell is Forever" (novelette, *Unknown Worlds*, August).

1946   Began writing for radio.

1950   Began writing for television and returned to writing science fiction.
        "The Devil's Invention" (story, later retitled "Oddy and Id," *Astounding*, August).

1951   "Of Time and Third Avenue" (story, *Fantasy and Science Fiction*, October).

1952   *The Demolished Man* (serial in *Galaxy* in January, February, and March).
        "Hobson's Choice" (story, *Fantasy and Science Fiction*, August).

1953   *The Demolished Man* (novel).
        Hugo Award for *The Demolished Man*.
        Who He? (novel, non-science fiction).
        "The Roller Coaster" (story, *Fantastic*, June).

"Star Light, Star Bright" (story, *Fantasy and Science Fiction*, July).

"Time is the Traitor" (story, *Fantasy and Science Fiction*, September).

"The Trematode, A Critique of Modern Science-Fiction" (essay, *The Best Science Fiction Stories: 1953*).

1954   Moved abroad and lived in Europe while working on *TSMD* and writing articles for *Holiday* magazine.

"5,271,009" (story, *Fantasy and Science Fiction*, March).

"Fondly Farenheit" (story, *Fantasy and Science Fiction*, August).

"Disappearing Act" (story, *New Worlds Science Fiction*, November).

1956   *The Stars My Destination* (serial in *Galaxy*, October, November, December, 1956; January, 1957).

Began writing a regular column for *Holiday*: "The Antic Arts: Television."

1957   "Science Fiction and the Renaissance Man" (lectue, delivered at University College, University of Chicago, February 22, 1957).

The Stars My Destination (novel).

1958   *Starburst* (collection of previously published stories, with the addition of "Travel Diary" and "The Die-Hard").

"The Men Who Murdered Mohammed" (story, *Fantasy and Science Fiction*, October).

1959   "Will You Wait?" (story, *Fantasy and Science Fiction*, March).

"The Pi Man" (story, *Fantasy and Science Fiction*, October).

1960   Began reviewing books for *Fantasy and Science Fiction* (October).

1961   An angry critique of science fiction and a composite picture of Bester's ideal science-fiction author in *Fantasy and Science Fiction* (February, March).

1962   Last book review column (July).

1963   "Epilogue: My Private World of Science Fiction" (essay, *The Worlds of Science Fiction*).

"They Don't Make Life Like They Used To" (novelette, *Fantasy and Science Fiction*, October).

1964   *The Dark Side of the Earth* (collection of previously published stories, with the addition of "Out of This World" and "The Flowered Thundermug").

1966   *The Life and Death of a Satellite* (non-fiction).

1967   Made Senior Literary Editor of *Holiday* (July).

1968   "Ms. Found in a Champagne Bottle" (story, *Status*).

1969   "How a Science Fiction Author Works" (essay, symposium in Brazil).

1970	Left *Holiday* when the magazine changed hands.
1972	"Writing and 'The Demolished Man' " (essay, *Algol*, May). "The Animal Fair" (story, *Fantasy and Science Fiction*, October).
1973	"Something Up There Likes Me" (story, *Astounding: John W. Campbell Memorial Anthology*).
1974	"The Four-Hour Fugue" (story, *Analog*, June). *The Indian Giver* (serial in *Analog*, November and December, 1974; January, 1975).
1975	*The Computer Connection* (novel, formerly serial, *The Indian Giver*, 1974). "My Affair with Science Fiction" (autobiographical essay).
1976	*The Light Fantastic: The Great Short Fiction of Alfred Bester* (collection of previously published short stories). *Star Light, Star Bright: The Great Short Fiction of Alfred Bester* (collection of previously published stories, an interview and an essay). *Starlight: The Great Short Fiction of Alfred Bester* (combined *The Light Fantastic* and *Star Light, Star Bright* in one volume). "Here Come the Clones" (story-essay, *Publishers Weekly*, July 14).
1979	"Galatea Galante" (story, *Omni*, April).
1980	*Golem*[100].

II

INTRODUCTION

Biography

Alfred Bester was born December 18, 1913, in Manhattan. Because his parents were "liberal and iconoclastic,"[1] he was allowed to choose his own beliefs: he chose "Natural Law"—since that time, he seems to have followed the laws of his own ebullient and energetic nature. Fantasy filled his early years; fairy tales were his favorite reading material until Hugo Gernsback's *Amazing* appeared in 1926. Lacking money to buy the issues, the young Bester would either borrow them or hang around the newsstands, reading as much as he could before being chased away by the proprietor, then return later and go through the same sequence of events. Although the stories enthralled him at first, he became increasingly frustrated with them:

> The pulp era had set in and most of the stories were about heroes with names like 'Brick Malloy,' who were inspired to combat space pirates, invaders from other worlds, giant insects and all the rest of the trash still being produced by Hollywood today.[2]

This youthful judgment has remained with the adult Bester, and he is still a harsh critic of melodramatic clichés in science fiction.

He graduated from the University of Pennsylvania in 1935, where he had tried to become a modern Renaissance Man,

> biting off more than I could chew, taking extra courses in psychology, music, art, and slipping my disk winning varsity letters. . . . I used to rush from the comparative anatomy lab to the art studio to my class in music composition and orchestration, trailing scents of formaldehyde, sulphur dioxide, and artgum erasers.[3]

Then he tried law school for a couple of years, not quite knowing what he really wanted to do. "After finishing school, I drifted into writing. Drift is the only word. Put any man at loose ends and he invariably starts to write a book."[4] One of the things he wrote was a science fiction short story. Because he remembered that one of the few bright spots in the Gernsbackian literary wasteland had been Weinbaum's "A Martian Odyssey," he submitted his story to Weinbaum's publisher, Standard Magazines. Two editors, Mort Weisinger and Jack Schiff, took the young writer under their wing and helped him rewrite "Diaz-X": Bester still believes their kindness resulted from their delight and amusement at discovering that he knew a great deal about Joyce's *Ulysses* (and apparently told all he knew). After revision, the story, retitled "The Broken Axiom," won a prize of $50.00 in a contest sponsored by *Thrilling Wonder Stories* (April, 1939). Bester has since often told the tale of interviewing Robert Heinlein many years later and finding that after Heinlein

8

wrote his first story, "Lifeline," he had considered submitting it to the same contest. But when Heinlein learned *Astounding* was paying a penny a word, he placed it there and was paid $70.00. Bester has never forgotten that, although he won the contest, Heinlein "beat" him out by $20.00.[5]

"The Broken Axiom," although mostly silly melodrama now, measured up to its contemporaries. Dr. John Halday is transported to a co-existent reality using the matter transmitter he has invented. He finds himself being interrogated by sentient creatures of "flaming brilliance" (even from the beginning, Bester favored imagery of light and fire), but he is rescued when his assistant reverses the transmitter and returns him to his own reality. Although the character and method (foolhardy scientist and invented machine) were already stock props, the other world, with its alien inhabitants, was much less so. The biographical blurb accompanying the story says of Bester, "If he had his choice of the arts to follow, he would without doubt, he says, select all seven—or however many there are."[6] This probably holds as true for Bester today as it did then and as it has over the years, since he has remained a person of catholic and wide-ranging interests.

In the next three years, there were thirteen more stories, which Bester has recently called "rotten" and claims to have completely forgotten.[7] However, these did lead to his attendance at regular lunches of several science-fiction writers of the late 1930's: Henry Kuttner, Edmond Hamilton, Otto Binder, Malcom Jameson, and Manley Wade Wellman.

In 1942, when comic books began to become popular, Bester's two mentors, Weisinger and Schiff, moved to that market and took Bester with them as a writer of comic book scenarios. He knew little, or even less, when he started, but he learned quickly. Also, "the comics gave me an ample opportunity to get a lot of lousy writing out of my system."[8] In the next few years, he wrote for *Superman, Captain Marvel, The Green Lantern,* and *The Star Spangled Kid* while his science fiction writing stopped completely.

Four years later, Bester's wife, an actress, mentioned to him that the radio show *Nick Carter* needed scripts. He took one of his comic book scenarios, rewrote it into a radio script, and had it accepted, although not without a great deal of confusion. He had forgotten to give his home address, and the studio spent weeks trying to locate him. By the time he was found, he was "a legend in the industry" and "launched as a hot-shot writer" before he'd even been hired.[9] At this point, he had already written "an opera that got 3½ stars in the *Daily News*, a play that was optioned and dropped, a miserable novel and one good slick story."[10] For the next four or five years, he wrote for many radio shows, including *Nick Carter, Charlie Chan, The Shadow, Treasury Agent, Nero Wolfe, Hercule Poirot, The Falcon, Harvest of Stars,* and the *Jimmy Melton Show.* He loved doing this work and spent hours at the 42nd Street library, researching with "magpie attention" for anything and everything that might offer story ideas.[11]

Around 1950, Bester began to write for television, including, briefly, *Tom Corbett, Space Cadet*. This he enjoyed much less: the financial and intellectual constraints of a mass, excessively commercial, medium appalled and outraged him. (Once he got into trouble for trying to write "original scripts" when he was supposed to be handing in "ordinary" ones.[12]) He returned—or fled—to science fiction, writing primarily for Tony Boucher and Mick McComas of *Fantasy and Science Fiction*. His first story after the eight-year hiatus, "Oddy and Id" (originally published as "The Devil's Invention") was accepted by John W. Campbell, Jr., whom Bester had admired for years because Campbell had "rescued [science fiction] from the abyss of space pirates, mad scientists, their lovely daughters wearing just enough clothes to satisfy the postal authorities, and alien friends. . . ."[13] Unfortunately, Campbell was by then preaching dianetics: Bester remained unconverted in their first and only meeting but did become convinced that "a majority of the science-fiction crowd, despite their brilliance, were missing their marbles. Perhaps that's the price that must be paid for brilliance."[14] "The Devil's Invention" (changed slightly so its character motivation would not interfere with L. Ron Hubbard's theories—Bester rewrote it before it was reprinted later, restoring its Freudian motivation) was the only one of Bester's stories to appear in *Astounding* until 1973 when, ironically, he was asked to contribute a story for an *Astounding* Campbell memorial anthology (he did so, despite his protests that he never had been one of Campbell's writers).[15]

Then Horace Gold asked Bester to write for *Galaxy*: out of their discussions came the basic plot for *TDM*, which was serialized in *Galaxy* before its publication as a full-length book. The novel won the very first Hugo ever awarded for a novel (1953).

In that same year, Bester took out his ire at the television world with a venomous novel, *Who He?* Later published in paperback as *The Rat Race*, the novel centers on Jordan Lennox, the writer for a television show, *Who He?*, a mixture of second-rate drama and comedy from a comic and ventriloquist (Bester had written—not happily—for Paul Winchell, and his fictional character is probably based on Winchell) and a game show that asks simple-minded questions ("What's another name for Santa Claus? Who he?"). Threatening letters are being sent to the show, and Lennox tries to find their author, revealing in his search the seamy and sordid activities behind the scenes of a slick television show. We meet the vacuous and egotistical stars, the scheming agent, the grasping and lecherous producers and directors, the alcoholics, and the mentally unstable. Lennox calls them "poison eaters" after the women of history who ate arsenic for their complexions until they were consuming enough to kill anyone else. "Mixed-up, neurotic, sick in the head. . . . You have to be sick to like this rat-race. The higher up you rise in the spiral, the more precarious your balance becomes. . . like a kid on ten foot stilts" (chapter 5).

We finally discover that it is Lennox himself who has been writing the letters when he goes on two-day drunks. He has two sides: one which grasps and stabs like everyone else in "the business," and another which is honest and passionate; the latter hates the former and wants to kill him. But this revelation comes too late to save Lennox's closest friend Sam who has been sucked into the filthy whirlpool and commits suicide. The novel ends happily (arguably, unbelievably so) when Lennox and his girlfriend leave New York City for a country home and he begins therapy.

This mainstream novel bears great resemblance to Bester's science fiction: as usual, we have frenzied activity as obsessed characters race from one scene to the next. Jordan Lennox, not surprisingly, resembles Ben Reich (this and *TDM* must have been written almost simultaneously), the good man gone bad because of his unconcious drives. Much of the dialogue could come from either *Who He?* or *TDM* (a scene in chapter 3, where Lennox and his girlfriend agree to disagree sounds very much like Ben Reich's and Lincoln Powell's squaring off). And certainly the pacing is similar, as is the end: Powell gets the girl and Reich gets therapy; Lennox gets both (Lennox seems to be the unified character that is split into Powell and Reich in *TDM*).

Also, both the protagonist and the occasional first-person narrator of *Who He?* bear great resemblance to Bester—both are probably autobiographical characters.

With the money made from *Who He?*, Bester quit television and left for Europe, where he and his wife lived for a few years. There he worked on *TSMD*, often contacting people back home when he needed material unavailable in European libraries. The novel was serialized in *Galaxy* in four installments between October, 1956, and January, 1957, and was published in book form in 1956 in England as *Tiger! Tiger!* and as the revision, *TSMD* in the United States, in 1957. It has since come to be considered a classic by many and has won high praise from most critics.

Shortly before Bester left for Europe, *Holiday* magazine had asked him to do a feature article on television because of the knowledge he had demonstrated in *Who He?*[16] When he returned to the United States, it was as a fulltime writer for the magazine with a monthly column on television (the first appeared in January, 1956). He eventually became Senior Literary Editor (July, 1967) and meanwhile nearly disappeared from science fiction until the early 1970's, after *Holiday* had changed publishers and relocated (1970). Although Bester was not writing much science fiction during this time, he was the regular reviewer for *Fantasy and Science Fiction* from October, 1960, to July, 1962.

Also, while writing for *Holiday*, he was a regular contributor to *Rogue* magazine with a column entitled "Bester's World" that covered subjects like Lee Strasberg's Actors' Studio and how entertainers handle sport fishing. In addition, he wrote for *McCall's, Status, Show,* and *Venture.*

The only science fiction from Bester during these years were two collections, mostly reprints of earlier stories: *Starburst* in 1958 (which added "Travel Diary" and "The Die-Hard") and *The Dark Side of the Earth* in

1964 (which added "Out of this World" and "The Flowered Thunder-mug"). This disappearance led to questions; a typical response was this one:

> Reality had become so colorful for me that I no longer needed the therapy of science fiction. And since the magazine imposed no constraints on me, outside of the physical requirements of professional magazine technique, I no longer needed a safety valve.[17]

And the assignments he had were exciting—interviews with entertainers and artists, trips to a variety of places for a variety of reasons.

Bester returned to the fold in 1972 with the publication of "The Animal Fair" in *Fantasy and Science Fiction*. *Holiday* had moved to Indianapolis two years before and, according to the editor's introduction to the story, Bester had taken "one look at that mighty metrop" and declined the invitation to go along. The editor was delighted that Bester had returned to "honest fiction writing."[18] And, by 1975, *Analog* was serializing *The Indian Giver* (later published as *The Computer Connection*). Two collections of his short stories (*The Light Fantastic* and *Star Light, Star Bright*) were published in 1976, then combined to form *Starlight: The Great Short Fiction of Alfred Bester*.

Writing in 1975, Bester indicated his wish to return "to my first love, my original love, science fiction. I hope it's not too late to rekindle the affair."[19] As of this writing, a new story, "Galatea Galante," has appeared, and another novel, *Golem*[100] (based on "The Four-Hour Fugue") will be published in the spring of 1980.[20] Whether the flames will reach the brilliance of his work of the 1950's remains to be seen, but at least Alfred Bester is once more doing what he can do so well.

Alfred Bester on Science Fiction

Bester started writing science fiction in 1939 but began feeling discouraged about the state of the genre before then. His cynicism has continued to the present, and his pronouncements have raised more than a few hackles (although his rejoinder would undoubtedly be that his are the raised hackles, that science-fiction writers do not do the job they should do, but that he still has hope they will).

Probably the most inflammatory statements were made in "Science Fiction and the Renaissance Man," an essay published in 1969, but based on a lecture delivered in 1957. Here, he argues that what is significant for a writer is his "Charm Quotient," those traits of personality or character that make a person interesting to others: "the important ingredient in the artist is not talent, technique, genius or luck—the important ingredient is himself."[21] It should be mentioned that this was coming from a Bester totally involved in the entertainment media; his examples in the essay are more often the likes of Rosemary Clooney or Rex Harrison rather than literary artists, *i.e.*, entertainers whose stock in trade is more often their charisma rather than their carefully honed talents. From there, he maintains that science fiction is

> a form of literature palatable only in our moments of leisure, calm, euphoria. It's not Escape Fiction; it's Arrest Fiction. I use the word 'arrest' in the sense of arresting or striking attention. . . to excite, stimulate, enlarge.[22]

Basing his judgment on his working life at that time (a daily battle with the dozens of people involved in television production), he contends that science fiction is not going to appeal to the reader who is exhausted from his workaday life because it is too removed from reality. Its unbelievability makes it readable only when the reader is out of touch with reality.

Most of the arguments in this essay have since fallen by the wayside, and Bester has not since elaborated or even repeated them. However, one criticism has echoed through his reviews and essays ever since: "Science fiction rarely, if ever, deals with genuine human emotions and problems."[23] Bester's anguished cry at his fellow science-fiction writers, often pained, often angry, has been delivered for more than twenty years. It has led him to heap praise almost worshipful upon Theodore Sturgeon, who is "the most perceptive, the most sensitive, and the most adult of science-fiction writers" because he "is not preoccupied with the gadgetry of science; he prefers to extrapolate the human being rather than the test tube."[24] Those colleagues who gave priority to plot or idea over character have been sternly reprimanded:

> We urge Mr. Blish, for the sake of his formidable talent, to abandon intellect and take to drink, drugs, seduction, crime, politics. . . anything that will shock him into experiencing the stresses that torture people, so that he will be able to write about them with the same lucid dedication which he presently reserves exclusively for science.[25]

Bester has often said that his own literary models included Dickens, Rabelais and Reade and that his own works, although not imitations of them, are attempts to bring the same life to fictional characters that they did. For Bester, as for these early writers, it is the character who counts, and any sacrifice of this prime directive to another aspect of fiction is idolatry.

This basic tenet has resulted in fairly regular tirades over the years directed at science-fiction's immaturity, and its writers who childishly over-simplify reality (intellectual, emotional, and technical). Science fiction, Bester has said, "demands extra-powerful depth and realism of character to offset the strangeness of outre backgrounds and unusual ideas." But, instead, it

> can tell the reader the melting point of a solid on Mercury, the freezing point of a gas on Neptune, the explosion point of a nova in Andromeda, but it has no idea of the melting point, the freezing

13

point and the explosion point of a human being.[26]

The result is a reliance on tools, robots, and gadgets.

Bester admits he does not read much science fiction, mainly because he finds so much of it simplistic and lacking in realistic characters. A partial reason for this distance is undoubtedly his own experience as a professional writer of all kinds. Often he has said (to the point of quoting himself), "I am a working writer, I am a working stiff, I am not an entirely science fiction writer—I am an *everything* writer. . . ."[27] Unlike many, even most, other important contributors to the field, Bester has by no means spent his whole life in it: his fiction, although arguably stronger than many works by more prolific authors, makes up only a miniscule part of the science-fiction canon, and his offerings have come slowly, often with long periods between when he has not been in contact with the field. So, to Bester, science fiction often seems a small and isolated area, removed from the larger world around it and suffering from this isolation. When asked in 1963 what he felt contemporary science fiction's greatest weaknesses were, he answered,

> As a rule it is written by people who know little else but the small world of science fiction; and read by people who read little else. There are exceptions, of course, but in general the readers and writers of science fiction have limited horizons.[28]

In later years, however, he has tempered this accusation with his belief that this is true of most writers in other popular areas as well, that most writers live in a small world of childish make-believe, that all Americans are, in fact, "sophisticated illiterates."[29]

Also, Bester's own experience as "an everything writer" has led to his own peculiar view of science fiction as an escape valve, a literary market to which he could submit innovative, satiric, and creative pieces that television and magazines had rejected for fear of losing their commercial audience. He still sees science fiction as being "mind-stretching," as

> the last remaining outpost of free literary expression and experiment in our damned conventional culture. You can try to say anything and say it in any style you please; no holds barred. But it's infested with too many adult adolescents who use it as an excuse for writing childish fantasy, and I hate them in the same way that I loathe adults who use the freedom and beauty and excitement of sexual relations for porn. Yes, I contemn most science fiction readers and authors (not all) because they're degenerating a medium for magnificent thought and imagination.[30]

And so the battle will no doubt continue as long as Bester retains his voice as, rather like the parent whose well-loved, most promising child has been molested, he tries to warn off and reform the offender. His pronouncements more often than not suggest a deeply personal involvement that betrays his love for science fiction. He may not be one of its most prolific contributors, but he remains one of its more fervent lovers.

Alfred Bester's Science Fiction

Alfred Bester is an anomaly even in the world of science fiction, which prides itself on individuality or eccentricity (depending on point of view). Science-fiction writers, in general, have for decades lunched together, written together, even slept together; most have made their livings as professional, full-time writers of science fiction (or wanted to do so). Not so with Bester; he is not a member of the inner circle. Despite this, two of his three novels and several of his shorter pieces have become classics, not because they are typical, but because they are atypical. Bester's early novels (*TDM* and *TSMD*) were forerunners of the New Wave before it was even a ripple: they are stylistically innovative (even in typography), heavily imagistic, and psychological. His fiction takes risks; when it fails, the result is apt to be ghastly (*TCC*, for instance). When it succeeds, "somehow it is all passion, fire, flamboyance, and endlessly recomplicated invention."[31] Brian Aldiss includes Bester in a list of madmen necessary for the development of the field.[32]

Reading Bester can be like looking at a firework pinwheel: constant activity, sparks shooting off in every direction, speed, vibrant color and image—and a feeling of losing one's breath. His plots are always scenic, with rapid changes of setting and character occurring every few pages, not unlike cinematic technique.[33] The last two chapters of *TSMD* have Gully Foyle jaunting all over time and space (often within only one sentence): in this instance, the flurry of activity works beautifully to suggest first, Gully's terror and last, his godlike power. But at other times, the cuts are so sudden that the reader loses patience and the thread of the plot. This is probably the major weakness of *TCC*: it's filled with so many characters and settings that change so rapidly, reading it is like looking at scenery moving by at the speed of light. Discrimination is lost, along with continuity of plot and sympathy for characters who do not stay around long enough to be familiar.

This pinwheel technique works particularly well for suspense and mystery (*TDM*, *TSMD*, "Fondly Fahrenheit") as the reader is pushed along the inevitable path to a solution at its end. However, many may find Bester's short stories more palatable, as space restrictions force a unity and coherence the greater length of a novel does not. There still is rapid scene change, but the characters remain constant; breathless speed still exists, but it is controlled by the continuity of character.

It is this pinwheel effect that has resulted in "pyrotechnic" evolving as the favorite critical word for Bester. Unfortunately, the fire does get out of control at times, and logic and sense are sacrificed for speed and dizzyingly vivid image.

One of Bester's more exasperated critics, Damon Knight, fired off this salvo:

> Dazzlement and enchantment are Bester's methods. His stories

never stand still a moment; they're forever tilting into motion, vee ing, doubling back, firing off rockets to distract you. The repet tion of the key phrase in 'Fondly Fahrenheit,' the endless rea pearances of Mr. Aquila in 'The Starcomber' are offered mockin ly: try to grab at them for stability, and you find they mea something new all the time. Bester's science is all wrong, h characters are not characters but funny hats: but you never notic he fires off a smokebomb, climbs a ladder, leaps from a trapez plays three bars of 'God Save the King,' swallows a sword an dives into three inches of water. Good Heavens, what more do yo want?[34]

Knight and others have wanted fewer scientific mistakes, for one thing Knight mentions the labeling of Olivia Presteign (*TDM*) as blind whei in fact, she does see—but in infra-red. And there is also the matter c Gully Foyle's trailing debris after him in space (Knight suggests tha maybe Bester thinks there are convection currents in the vacuum c space). What is more likely is that Bester was more interested in th metaphor of a blind Olivia and in the image of Gully as a comet than i scientific accuracy.

Bester is generally unconcerned with science, accurate or inaccurate In a question-answer session at Seacon, 1979, Bester said: "I *hate* har science fiction" and went on to explain that he is not even faintly ii terested in science fact and formula and will happily make it up as h goes along; his concern is people, and the science, valid or invalid, is mere convenience to place people into stress situations.

And this is, without doubt, Bester's towering strength in science fic tion where idea or plot usually takes precedence over character. Fc Bester, character is first. And the memorable aspects of Bester's work are seldom ideas[35] or even plotting, but the people. How, exactly, Be Reich (*TDM*) murders and is captured may be of far less significanc than Ben himself, battling with all his wits to escape from his ow deranged self. What Gully Foyle (*TSMD*) does to exact revenge stand out less than Gully himself, the mad, driven beast. Blaise Skiaki an Gretchen Nunn ("The Four-Hour Fugue") are involved in a peculia mystery, but what fascinates is their characters, not the mystery. I most, or at least too much, science fiction, plot is all, and discussions c works often disintegrate into synopses. This is simply and emphaticall not true of Bester's works—a plot summary would not enlighten (might even confuse) without analysis of the people in the plot.

One of Bester's favorite character types is the obsessive, the perso driven by internal needs not even the character himself understands. Be Reich and Gully Foyle are obvious examples of this type. Aldis: paraphrased earlier, calls Bester mad—so are Bester's characters. In th novels and short stories, insanity, or an insane aberration, is often th motivation, as evidenced by James Vandaleur ("Fondly Fahrenheit" Blaise Skiaki ("The Four-Hour Fugue"); Peter Marko ("The Pi Man" Jeffrey Halsyon ("5,271,009"); and John Strapp ("Time is th

16

'raitor''). Even those who lack the obvious symptoms of lunacy are not quite normal—often because they wish for something they can't have, like Addyer, the mousey statistician in "Hobson's Choice," or Henry Hassel, the brilliant scientist in "The Men Who Murdered Mohammed." Bester's people learn to behave rationally (or are forced to by others, like Ben Reich or Jeffrey Halsyon), and perhaps there is hope in this—few manage to destroy themselves or their world (Odysseus Gaul in "Oddy and Id" is an obvious exception). But surely, no contemporary besides Sturgeon has shown the concern for the human predicament that Bester has. Younger writers, like Malzberg with his mad astronauts or Dick with his demented future citizens, may well have learned from Bester.

Another indicator of Bester's people priority is the lack of aliens in any of his works. Only in TCC does an alien briefly appear—and it seems to be non-sentient. If "alien" should be applied to any of his all-too-human characters, it may be to the women, who often are sterotypical females clinging to their men. Barbara D'Courtney and Mary Noyes (TDM) are particulary horrible examples who cling like love-lorn adolescents to Lincoln Powell who, stereotypically male, usually has better things to do. Stronger women are found in later works, like Jisbella McQueen (TSMD), Gretchen Nunn ("The Four-Hour Fugue"), or Florinda Pot ("Something Up There Likes Me"). Jisbella is a street-fighter, quite capable of caring for herself: her attraction to Gully is not schoolgirl romanticism but adult lust. Gretchen Nunn is a more-than-competent professional with her own career, and so is Florinda Pot. They both become involved with men, but the relationships seem to be interdependent, rather than the traditional woman dependent on the man. The difference between the women of earlier works (the 1950's) and those of the later (the 1970's) may well result from the time frame itself and its effects on Bester's perception and awareness. In fact, Bester seems far less the male chauvinist than his contemporaries of the 1950's who produced a literature that did not stereotype the female because it did not often include her. Most of Bester's works in more recent years do include strong female characters.

Also it seems evident from an overall look at Bester's fiction that there is a priority on pairing and bonding. All three of his novels end happily with couples pairing off (Powell and Barbara in TDM; Robin Wednesbury and Y'ang Yeovil, Jisbella McQueen and Saul Dagenham in TSMD; Natoma Guess and Edward Curzon in TCC). Several of the short stories end the same way ("The Pi Man"; "The Four-Hour Fugue"; "Galatea Galante"). At times, in his fiction, the pairing seems forced (in the novels, especially), but that it happens at all makes Bester's stories different from his contemporaries' and their lone heroes.

And the happy endings may well result from what Bester read and admired so long ago—the classical masters, Dickens in particular, whose endings have often been criticized as sentimental and forced. Mainstream classic writers (pre-twentieth century) usually emphasized the need for a return to order by the end of a work; Bester's works demonstrate this principle. Almost every novel and story ends on a note of affirmation and restored order ("Fondly Fahrenheit" and "Star Light, Star Bright" are obvious exceptions). Occasionally this seems imposed (the somewhat ponderous philosophising at the end of TDM and TSMD, for instance) but the action of disorder has been reordered by the end.

By the time order has been restored, we have vivid memories of the images by which the tale has been told. Few science-fiction writers have relied on the vividly concrete image as much as Bester. His ficton is filled to overflowing (sometimes literally, when the imagery is vivid but irrelevant to theme or plot) with color, shape, texture, and temperature. Flames and light appear in nearly every work, but so do places (the orchidlike murder room and the melted ceramics factory of TDM), faces (Gully's burning tiger mask), things (the elephant in the living room or the musical termitelike cryonauts of TCC), even the mixture of all senses (Gully's experience of synaesthesia). Surely Bester's are among the most imagery-laden works until those of much younger writers (Delany and Zelazny for example).

Last, we must consider Bester's wit; few of his works function in a humorless universe, and a great part of his skill is the irony and satire found in his fiction. The philosophizing near the end of TSMD referred to above has been seen by some as ponderous, but the philosophizing is coming from a robot whose circuits have been "disrupted" by radiation (i.e., from an unbalanced or insane robot); surely this is intended to be on one level at least, funny (Gully Foyle, who has listened to no one, finally takes the word of a mad robot). Bester has also consistently deflated science-fiction clichés through his years of writing: the second Adam and Eve plot; the superman character; the time machine ploy; the sentient machine. Part of that order, which is restored at the end of most works, results in no small part from this deflation and wit (the world has been lost to a dictator in both "Something Up There Likes Me" and "Oddy and Id," but somehow, this seems more amusing than tragic, thanks to the whimsical tone). The absurdity of life is made manifest in Bester—and this is a matter for laughter, not tears.

These are the qualities that make Bester not only readable, but definable as at least superb craftsman, possibly as artist—his manic but human characters and the vividness and wit with which they are portrayed. For these, if nothing else, he deserves high praise and his fiction deserves to be read and reread.

1. Alfred Bester, "My Affair with Science Fiction," Hell's Cartographers (New York: Harper & Row, 1975), p. 46.

2. Bester, p. 48.

3. Alfred Bester, quoted in "Alfred Bester," The Human Equation: Short Novels of Tomorrow, ed. William F. Nolan, (Los Angeles: Sherbourne Press, 1971), pp. 2-3.

4. Alfred Bester, "Science Fiction and the Renaissance Man," The Science Fiction Novel (Chicago: Advent, 1969), p. 78.

5. "Interview with Robert Heinlein," Algol, November 1973, pp. 32-33.

6. Meet the Author of This Prize Story," *Thrilling Wonder Stories*, April 1939, p. 64.

7. Bester, "My Affair," pp. 49-50.

8. Bester, "My Affair," p. 54.

9. Alfred Bester, quoted in "Who and Where," *Holiday*, October 1964, p. 33.

10. Alfred Bester, "Writing the Radio Mystery," *Writer*, December 1951, p. 391. He also added in this article that "Radio isn't a rat-race unless you've got a rat-race in your own mind. If you've crawled around through pulp and stumbled around in the slicks, try a brisk walk through AM [radio]. It'll put you on your feet technically and financially, and prepare you for your first flight into literature.

"Beyond that I can't advise you. I'm too busy worrying about that flight myself," (p. 395).

11. Bester, "My Affair," p. 55.

12. Bester, "My Affair," p. 56.

13. Bester, "Science Fiction and the Renaissance Man," p. 79.

14. Bester, "My Affair," p. 60.

15. Alfred Bester, "Something Up There Likes Me," *Starlight: The Great Short Fiction of Alfred Bester* (Garden City, New York: Nelson Doubleday, 1976), p. 363.

16. Alfred Bester, "Inside TV," *Holiday*, October 1954, pp. 54-61, 79-80, 82-86.

17. Bester, 'My Affair," p. 69.

18. *Fantasy and Science Fiction*, October 1972, p. 5.

19. Bester, "My Affair," p. 69.

20. Letter received from Alfred Bester, 7 November 1979.

21. Bester, "Science Fiction and the Renaissance Man," p. 81.

22. Bester, "Science Fiction and the Renaissance Man," p. 86.

23. Bester, "Science Fiction and the Renaissance Man," p. 94.

24. Alfred Bester, "Books," *Fantasy and Science Fiction*, March 1961, p. 78.

25. Alfred Bester, "Books," *Fantasy and Science Fiction*, December 1960, p. 71.

26. Alfred Bester, "The Trematode, A Critique of Modern Science-Fiction," *The Best Science-Fiction Stories: 1953*, ed. Everett F. Bleiler and T. E. Dikty (New York: Frederick Fell, 1953), pp. 17-18.

27. Alfred Bester, "How a Science Fiction Author Works," *SF Symposium* (Rio de Janeiro: Instituto Nacional do Cinema, 1969), p. 122.

28. Alfred Bester, Response to questionnaire, *The Double: Bill Symposium*, ed. Bill Mallardi and Bill Bowers (Akron, Ohio: D.B. Press, 1969), p. 101.

29. Alfred Bester, "Alfred Bester," Interview by Darrell Schweitzer, *Science Fiction Voices (Baltimore, Md.: T-K Graphics, 1976), pp. 6-7.

30. Letter from Alfred Bester.*

31. Samuel Delany, "Introduction," *The Cosmic Rape* by Theodore Sturgeon (Boston: Gregg, 1977), p. ix.

32. Brian Aldiss, "Introduction," *Galactic Empires* (New York: St. Martin's Press, 1976), II, viii.

33. Why none of Bester's novels has been filmed remains a mystery. *TDM* was bought and adapted by Alexander Jacobs in 1968, but never made. Jacobs blames this on Hollywood's fear of "films with ideas." Andrew Laskos, "The Greatest Movies Never Made," *American Film*, September 1979, p. 52.

34. *In Search of Wonder* (Chicago, Advent, 1967), p. 234.

35. He once told an interviewer, "I'm in the entertainment business. I leave the messages to Western Union." *Speaking of Science Fiction: The Paul Walker Interviews* (New York: Luna, 1978), p. 313.

III.

THE DEMOLISHED MAN

Alfred Bester's *The Demolished Man* was published in 1953 to the accompaniment of rave reviews. P. Schuyler Miller, reviewing it in *Astounding*, predicted it would become a classic—he was right. Carl Sagan, in a *New York Times* article, "Growing Up with Science Fiction" (May 28, 1978), included *The Demolished Man* in a list of his favorite works:

> stories that are so tautly constructed, so rich in the accomodating details of an unfamiliar society that they sweep me along before I have a chance to be critical.

The novel, "a touchstone of hybrid SF and detective fiction," according to Neil Barron's *Anatomy of Wonder* (Bowker, 1976, p. 141), traces the predicament and tragedy of Ben Reich, an "interplanetary tycoon" who feels backed into a corner by the D'Courtney Cartel, a competitive organization. Reich's distress takes the form of nightmares about a "Man with No Face," and he sends off a coded telegram to Craye D'Courtney, suggesting a merger of their two financial empires. When Reich mistakenly believes his offer has been rejected, he kills his archrival. The rest of the novel centers on the cat and mouse game played by Reich and Lincoln Powell, a telepathic Police Prefect who discovers that Reich has killed his own father.

Although the society in which Lincoln Powell pursues Ben Reich is not fully developed, it is both futuristic and fantastic. The glimpses we have of it reveal a way of life both sensual and deadening—a kind of moral hedonism attractive, perhaps, on the surface, but lethal to the spirit. William Godshalk, writing in the May, 1975, issue of *Extrapolation*, took a harshly critical look at *The Demolished Man* in an article entitled, "Alfred Bester: Science Fiction or Fantasy?" He noted a high level of illogic and exaggeration, concluding that the novel is both comic and a parody of the conventions of science fiction. Certainly Bester's social settings are outrageous, but they do not parody literature; rather, they satirize a contempory reality. Groff Conklin perceptively commented in his *Galaxy* review of *The Demolished Man* 25 years ago that

> one is given a violently real view of a society in which the neuroses of 20th century urbanism have been almost infinitely multiplied through extrapolation.

The society is an exaggerated one, but its purpose is more than simple entertainment.

The murder takes place at Maria Beaumont's party (chapter 4), a gathering of *la dolce vita* at its futuristic best. Reich is able to buy himself an invitation by sending the hostess an antique book accompanied by an appraisal of its worth ("as was the custom": in this society, one does not

20

only look a gift horse in the mouth, one counts its teeth). Maria's invitation and thank you note is appropriately gushy—"sweet," "divine," —and arrives with a nude portrait of herself set in a synthetic ruby. The party itself makes those excesses seem petty. Fittingly, Maria's Beaumont House is a replica of the Baths of Caracalla of ancient and decadent Rome. Caracalla was a second-century Roman emperor known both for his extravagant tastes that depleted the empire's coffers and for his admirable ability to murder any of his family members he saw as a threat to him or his throne. Although he did not kill his father, he was suspected of trying to hasten his father's demise. He makes a suitable role model for both Maria Beaumont and Ben Reich.

The party sounds like a 1970's disco gone mad, with flashing lights beaming from the groined vault ceiling (as a reinforcing image of death and decay) turning the gaudy display of costumes to a variety of colors. Some guests wear ultra-violet windows in their outfits so that pertinent body parts seem to appear and disappear as the lights change (this may be the one part of the novel where the reader rather likes Ben Reich, who shows up in an opaque suit). Maria Beaumont has been "transformed by pneumatic surgery into an exaggerated East Indian figure with puffed hips, puffed calves and puffed gilt breasts" (chapter 4)—a sort of caricature of Elizabeth Taylor in one of her fat periods. She is surrounded by effete secretaries whose major abilities seem to be "peeping" (telepathically eavesdropping) and gushing. And her character is only slightly less appealing than her appearance. A gatecrasher is discovered but, as he wants her photograph and, as her secretary lewdly suggests, "he'd like to steal more from you than your picture" (chapter 4), Maria allows him to stay. Lest we feel any attraction to this bloated body and ego, Maria "cackles" and "squawks" her lines of dialogue. Her enemies, Ben Reich recalls, have nicknamed her "The Gilt Corpse"—a name that, like Caracalla, pairs wealth and death. Later, Reich is able to kill D'Courtney because of Maria's vast enthusiasm for the game in the book he has sent her: called "Sardine," it it a version of "Hide and Seek," to which Maria has added the fillip of nudity, displaying her own "astonishing nude body" first—while lights fade from the dais on which she is standing.

Other forms of entertainment for the idle rich can be found at Spaceland, the future's Disneyworld, where the pampered jet set (rocket set?) wear painted-on clothes and indulge in revival meetings, bathe in a variety of sulphur springs, play free-flight polo, or spend time at the Plastic Surgery Resort (chapter 12). Bester caps this brief description of a Roman emperor's delight with an Evelyn Waugh description of the future's idea of religious observance: a replica of Notre Dame Cathedral labeled, with obvious irony, "Ye Wee Kirk O Th' Glen," where a gargoyle's syrupy voice announces that a ticket to "this sacred exhibit" will gain the viewer a show of robots portraying "the drama of the gods"—Moses, Christ, Mohammed, Lao Tse, and Mary Baker Eddy are haphazardly mixed in the attraction. Lincoln Powell collapses in laughter, and the reader is inclined to follow suit.

For those with similar tastes (or lacking them), the society of 2301 offers Chooka Frood's (chapter 9), where opportunities to satiate old and new vices (called "frabs") are provided. This funhouse labyrinth, the remains of a ceramics plant fused and splashed by wartime explosions, has the atmosphere of a pyschedelic whorehouse that comes complete with crystal balls (Chooka is a medium). Also offered in this chapter is the kinky scene of a blind man fondling a young woman while his wife describes the scene to him.

These quick glimpses of a corrupt and hedonistic society suggest a chaotic and disordered world, spiritually dead—like The Gilt Corpse. The two protagonists move through these scenes: one in his attempt to capture, the other in his attempt to escape. Ben Reich, the deranged murderer, seems to fit into these scenes—they, like him, are mad; Lincoln Powell does not fit. The party he has at his home early in the novel (chapter 2) offers a strong contrast to the entertainment indulged in by the rest of the world. Powell's party consists of conversation, food, drink, and laughter where people rely on one another's wits for pleasure, rather than on bizarre games, scenery, and costumes intended to titillate jaded palates.

However, the most intriguing part of this society is, of course, its telepathic element. Bester postulates a world where some people are gifted with the ability to read others' thoughts. These espers (called "peepers" colloquially) belong to the Esper Guild, an organization rather like a law board or the AMA, designed to locate latent espers, define and enforce esper ethics, educate telepaths, and enforce a genetic plan (espers can marry only other espers). Each esper is tested, trained, and assigned a rank of one to three, depending on the strength of his/her abilities. Esper "ones" have the most powerful talent and are usually doctors, psychiatrists, policemen, etc. Brief scenes in the novel show us more about this aspect of the society. Although these scenes are not organically necessary to the plot, they do sketch in a realistic background for the Powell-Reich battle.

The espers of The Demolished Man are clearly the positive forces of their society—their guild even has a pledge reminiscent of the Hippocratic Oath, promising mutual support and use of their talents "for the benefit of mankind" (chapter 7). Only three of the espers in the novel are corrupt. One of them, Chooka Frood, is only a latent peeper. Augustus Tate is corrupted by Ben Reich but finally sees the error of his ways and promises to aid Powell shortly before he is killed in a harmonic gun attack. Jerry Church was ostracized years before by the Guild for unethical actions; he is consistently associated with shadows and his mental suffering is clear—he too finally agrees to help Powell.

The telepathic element adds to the excitement of the pursuit, but it also underlines and emphasizes the theme of the novel: the necessity for knowledge of one's identity. Bester tells us, both at the beginning and the end of the work, that

> In the endless universe there has been nothing new, nothing dif-
> ferent. What has appeared exceptional to the minute mind of man
> has been inevitable to the infinite Eye of God. This strange second
> in a life, that unusual event, those remarkable coincidences of en-
> vironment, opportunity, and encounter. . .all of them have been
> reproduced over and over on the planet of a sun whose galaxy
> revolves once in two hundred million years and has revolved nine
> times already (chapter 17).

There is nothing new under the sun: society may change, but its people
know and will continue to know the same pains and joys that people
before have known.

The novel is basically a retelling of the Oedipus myth—certainly this
takes no great perception: Barron's *Anatomy of Wonder* mentions it,
even the publisher's blurb on the paperback edition repeats this. But
Bester's novel deals with the myth in more depth than just the unwitting
murder of a father by his son. Ben Reich, like Oedipus, does not know
who he is (in a larger sense than just parentage), is arrogant in his supposed wisdom, and overweening in his pride. Lincoln Powell is Reich's
other half—the seeker who sees more clearly and learns Reich's terrible
secret after determined, even obsessive, pursuit and search.

Ben Reich is Oedipus Rex: his last name means, in German, "empire"
or "kingdom"; the firm he heads is Monarch Utilities and Resources,
Inc. Like the original king, Reich is exceedingly clever. Despite the fact
that he lacks esper ability, he plans and executes a murder in a society
where murder has been considered impossible for 70 years. The first and
third chapters show us his carefully planned scheme. He manages to pro-
cure an antique gun in a world where all guns have been consigned to
museums (and his weapon almost causes the police case to collapse until
Powell finally realizes what must have been used and how). Reich is not
an esper, but he does have an almost telepathic ability to sense
weaknesses in others so that he can devise the proper bribe—for
Augustus Tate, power over the Esper Guild; for Jerry Church, a chance
at reinstatement; for Maria Beaumont, a new game to enliven her party;
for Duffy Wyg&, a little feigned interest in her skills as a jingle writer.
The appearance of an unexpected esper 2 at the crucial party is handled
by Reich's distracting him—again, locating his weakness and feeding it
(flattery from the great financier and Maria's photographs so he can
prove to friends he was at the party). In Reich's desperate attempts to
foil Powell, he bribes and manipulates so successfully that Powell admits
defeat at least twice: "Damn it, we're licked!" (chapter 8).

The mythic Oedipus was a man of great will and tyrannizing strength
(Oedipus Tyrannus is, of course, another name for him), capable of
single-handedly killing his father and several attendants in a fit of rage
because he had been forced off the road. Ben Reich also possesses this
tyrannical rage as evidenced by several incidents. The opening scene
shows Reich awakening from yet another nightmare of The Man with No

Face; when his servant tells him he has been screaming loudly in terror, Reich swears at him and orders him out. A few pages later he arrives at his office in a foul mood and brusquely orders out his secretary and her staff:

> "Dump it and jet," he growled.
> They deposited the papers and recording crystals on his desk and departed hastily, but without rancor. They were accustomed to his rages (chapter 1).

And the first time Powell meets Reich, he (Reich) is described as "Tall, broad-shouldered, determined, exuding a tremendous aura of charm and power. There was kindliness in that power, but it was corroded by the habit of tyranny" (chapter 6). Like Oedipus, Reich has those qualities of the ruler for whom power has become ends rather than means.

Reich's overweening arrogance evinces itself as well. Oedipus was sure he knew everything and could overcome all odds: so is Reich. Like Oedipus, like the classical murderer Raskolnikov, Reich sees himself as omnipotent. In the introductory scene, Reich admires himself in the mirror and murmurs, "I wouldn't change looks with the devil. I wouldn't change places with God" (chapter 1). As the plot progresses, Reich's madness grows and so does his delusion of himself as godlike. After Powell has nearly succeeded in cornering him, Reich screams that Powell is "trying to nail me to the D'Courtney cross. . ." (chapter 14). When Powell tells him that he is free for lack of a motive, Reich exults in triumph, seeing himself as a primeval hunter:

> I'll complete the picture with Powell's head. . .stuffed and mounted on my wall. I'll complete the picture with the D'Courtney Cartel stuffed into my pockets. By God, give me time and I'll complete a picture with the Galaxy inside the frame (chapter 15).

Reich is finally brought to Demolition through a mass linking with all the espers, channeled through Lincoln Powell who creates for Reich a fantasy world. The fantasy begins in Duffy Wyg&'s apartment where Ben Reich offers Duffy the galaxy if she wants it: "Want to look at God? Here I am. Go ahead and look" (chapter 16).

The horror of this vision is its at least partial truth. Reich's successful murder of D'Courtney would result in his practically being owner of the universe. Between his financial empire and D'Courtney's, he would have a godlike power. Since Ben Reich is insane and self-destructive, the effect of his power may well have been a mad world, intent on destroying itself. The plight of Oedipus involved not only his own life, but the life of the society he ruled—Oedipus's crime is reflected in, and cause of, the blight on Thebes: the dying crops, cattle, and children. Bester has shown us in *The Demolished Man* a society that is already decadent and perhaps spiritually dead. Reich's control would surely have destroyed it completely. Only Powell perceives this, as he explains to Commissioner Crabbe after Reich has been safely packed off to Kingston Hospital (the name was undoubtedly selected for Reich), ". . .he was in a position of power to rock the solar system. He was one of those rare World-Shakers whose compulsions might have torn down our society and irrevocably committed us to his own psychotic pattern" (chapter 17).

Reich does not marry his mother, who is long since dead when the novel opens. But the murder scene (chapters 4 and 5) contains more than a subtle hint of blighted sexuality, to which attention is drawn through repetition and emphasis. Maria Beaumont's party and she herself establish a background of exaggerated and repulsive sexuality. On his way to D'Courtney's room, Reich fends off a naked woman who has grabbed him. He enters the murder room by a door set between two panels—the Rape of Lucrece and the Rape of the Sabine Women (continuing the Roman references, as well as suggesting a perverted sexuality)—which leads into an anteroom and thence into

> . . .a spherical room designed as the heart of a giant orchid. The walls were curling orchid petals, the floor was a golden calyx; the chairs, tables, and couches were orchid and gold. But the room was old. The petals were faded and peeling; the golden tile floor was ancient and the tesselations were splitting (chapter 4).

This is the wedding suite of the Beaumont House—logically, an odd place to put an elderly man dying of cancer, but ironically and symbolically, an ideal place for a bastard son to kill the father who did not legitimize his birth. Both the layout (an anteroom and a spherical inerior room) and the shape (orchid) suggest an entry into a vagina and uterus, in this case, an aged vagina and uterus. Jeff Riggenback, in "Science Fiction as Will and Idea: The World of Alfred Bester" (*Riverside Quarterly*, August 1972), notes this imagery and comments that "in Freudian theory the father is seen by the son as despoiler of the mother." Another point of view, sustained by the imagery, is that Ben Reich has come to rape and destroy, perhaps even to abort. Since we know, in retrospect, that the Man with No Face is both Reich and his father D'Courtney (for so Reich sees the figure in his last coherent vision: "Two faces blending into one. Ben D'Courtney. Craye Reich. D'Courtney-Reich"—chapter 16), the victim of Reich's murder is both his father and himself. Reich commits both parricide and his own desired suicide. In killing his father, he tries to kill himself.

Reich is "saved" by Lincoln Powell—i.e., his physical life is spared, but his psychic life is torn down, to be built up again. The word "demolish" does mean "destroy," but it comes from two Latin roots: *de*, down, and *moliri*, to build or construct; thus, its current definition plus its etymology provides the meaning here: a tearing down to be built up.

Godshalk, in his article in *Extrapolation* (see secondary bibliography), has already noted that "Powell is the acceptable father of the novel." Both his name (Lincoln) and his title (Prefect) suggest leadership and discipline. As Godshalk points out, Powell is seen by both women who love him as a father. Mary Noyes, whose love is unrequited, thinks to him, "*I love you. Image of my father: Symbol of security: Of warmth: Of protecting passion. . .*" (chapter 2). When Barbara D'Courtney reverts to infancy as a result of the trauma of seeing her father murdered, she must re-grow-up, a process taking three weeks. During that time, she sees Powell as her father, promising to marry him when she grows up. When he peeps her, he encounters his own image in her psyche, at first connected with the words "Papa" and "Father," then as part of a Janus-headed figure with her real, biological father (chapter 11). At the very end of the novel, Barbara has grown up, Powell realizes he loves her, and the two plan to marry. The incest of the original Oedipus has been reworked: Bester's tale has a father marrying his daughter, rather than a son marrying his mother. Powell is a successful Oedipal figure (or an Agamemnon?).

Godshalk comments on the "strange union throughout between the killer and his pursuer." This union exists because Oedipus was both detective and criminal; Bester has split the two so Powell and Reich are halves of the same whole. This is suggested when the two first meet and share an instant rapport. Although he is not a telepath, Reich knows that Powell has tried to peep him, despite his promise not to: "It's what I would have done," he tells Powell (chapter 6). The two of them agree that neither one of them is very trustworthy, and Reich comments to the man he has just met, "We play for keeps, both of us" (chapter 6). Powell tells Reich that he intends "to strangle the lousy killer in you," that this "is the beginning of the end for you. You know it." Reich wavers for a moment, "on the verge of surrender," but finally accepts the challenge: "And give up the best fight of my life? No. Never in a million years, Linc. We're going to slug this out straight down to the finish." The two shake hands as Reich remarks, "I lost a great partner in you," and they agree to be enemies (chapter 6).

Powell retains his admiration for Reich throughout. When, midway through the investigation, Mary Noyes calls Reich "a disgusting, dangerous man," Powell corrects her: "Dangerous but not disgusting, Mary. He's got charm" (chapter 10).

The mass cathexis that psychologically links Powell and Reich simply makes obvious what has been suggested: the two become one as Powell, in God-the-father fashion, shapes a world for Reich. The two are found together the next moring: ". . .both were drawn inevitably together like two magnetized needles floating on a weed-choked pond" (chapter 17). At the very end of the novel, Powell offers Reich, who is by then a "gibbering, screaming, twitching," "naked thing," some candy and is staggered by the response he receives. "Out of the chaos in Reich came an explosive fragment: '*Powell-peeper-Powell-friend-Powell-friend*' " (chapter 17). Powell's eyes fill with tears, and he is clearly very moved. It is as if the demented side of himself has had a moment of sanity and wants to thank that half that helped. A moment before, Powell had seen himself and "all of us" (all espers) as nothing but "nursemaids to this

26

crazy world" and wondered if it were worth it. After Reich's response, he cries, in thought:

> Listen normals! You must learn what it is. You must learn how it is. You must tear the barriers down. You must tear the veils away. We see the truth you cannot see. . .That there is nothing in man but love and faith, courage and kindness, generosity and sacrifice. All else is only the barrier of your blindness. One day we'll all be mind to mind and heart to heart (chapter 17).

Although this end could be accused of sententiousness, its optimism overrides this. The lesson of Oedipus that western civilization always found is that of the value of seeing, of perception, of awareness. In *The Demolished Man* the same lesson is implicit and explicit in Powell's final speech. Seeing is all, and when we can perceive all people and see them all clearly, then, even the criminal can be realized as containing a basic good. And what better image to use for the importance of perception than that of telepathy?

IV

THE STARS MY DESTINATION

When *The Stars My Destination* first appeared (in England as *Tiger! Tiger!* in 1956 and revised with its present title here in 1957), it received mixed reviews. Critics praised its invention and originality, but objected to its violence, it scientific errors, and even its inclusion of sex (this last element was one aspect of human life that science fiction had remained innocent of until the 1960's). However, by the time a hardcover edition came out in 1975, a few critics still objected to the novel's exaggerations (e.g., Gully's obsession), but most seemed to admire it more than their predecessors 18 years before. Much of what seemed unacceptable, even shocking, in the 1950's seemed tolerable, even praiseworthy, in the 1970's. Perhaps the times are beginning to catch up with the novel.

In Gully Foyle of *The Stars My Destination*, Bester has created another obsessive-compulsive world-shaker like Ben Reich. Unlike Ben Reich, however, Gully does not remain the same throughout. When *TDM* ends, we are given a strong hint that the demolition may result in Reich's rehabilitation. But Gully's rehabilitation begins earlier and is self-engendered and self-motivated. If the protagonists of *The Stars My Destination* and *TDM* were to be compared, *The Stars My Destination* might be seen as the stronger of the two works because Gully is a dynamic character, a sinner who saves himself, rather than a criminal like Reich who is saved from himself, despite himself.

Bester, in "My Affair with Science Fiction," mentions that *The Stars My Destination* began with

> the notion of using the *Count of Monte Cristo* pattern for a story. The reason is simple; I'd always preferred the anti-hero and I'd always found high drama in compulsive types.

Gully, like Dumas' Edmund Dantes, is unjustly condemned to imprisonment and eventual death but succeeds in escaping through his own cleverness and ability; his quest for vengeance leads him to wealth and social position and to superhuman abilities through a system of implants, as well as the vengeance he seeks. But Bester does Dumas one better with his anti-hero: Gully reaches the deepest pits of human bestiality, then begins to develop a morality. In a way, the novel is one of maturation as its hero grows up to civilized, moral adulthood. Gully the brute becomes a human being. Gully the tiger is reborn as a lamb. William Blake's poem suggests one god made both creatures; Bester's novel suggests that both reside within one human being.

The novel places great emphasis upon redemption, good developing from evil. It is filled to overflowing with horrible examples of cruelty and betrayal; those involving Gully may be among the more memorable, but almost every character in the book either betrays or is betrayed, after which retribution is sought. In many cases, the payment is destruction. As Saul Dagenham, the most scarred (literally) and the wisest character, says, "There's no defense against betrayal. . ." (chapter 12). Yet, most of the time, payment is eventually exacted and good returns (at least enough to balance out the evil). The crucial betrayal is, of course, the *Vorga*'s bypassing the shipwrecked Gully. The ship's name reminds us of "Borgia," a name synonymous with self-serving brutality and murder. Also, Gully and Robin wear New Year's Eve costumes of Cesare and Lucrezia Borgia (chapter 10), and Presteign tells Olivia that Fourmyle looks "like a Borgia" (chapter 12). One of the central ironies of the novel is that Gully, in his blind drive for revenge, becomes Borgia-like, himself developing the cruelty that he has seen the *Vorga* as embodying. The *Vorga* speeds by Gully because its refugees, who believe they have been rescued and are escaping to Earth, are going to be betrayed—jettisoned into space after they have been looted for valuables. Kempsey tells Gully much later that 600 were jettisoned; his description of the looting and panic could be of a scene from a concentration camp (chapter 12). The similarity of *Vorga*'s betrayal of six hundred to the Holocaust's destruction of six million cannot be accidental. The corpses from the gas ovens were probed for valuables, as the *Vorga* passengers were looted. Later, when Jisbella discovers Gully took keys from the pocket of the dead Sam Quatt, she screams "Ghoul!" at him (chapter 6) and will not speak to him for days afterwards—Gully, like the *Vorga*, sacrifices humanity to greed.

However, it is comforting to see that Bester has exacted payment for his war criminals: one has become a psychotic addicted to a drug (Forrest—chapter 9); another has gone mad (Kempsey and his clothes phobia which makes him an outcast, even among outcasts—chapter 12); and the ship's captain has submitted to an operation that has deadened all her senses and remanded her to a living death in a monastery more like a tomb (chapter 13). The genocide of World War II and the *Vorga*'s scuttling refugees represent a total betrayal of humanity for which retribution must be made. We do not know what, if any, punishment Olivia pays (aside from Gully's rejection of her), but Bester has already ensured her crew's punishment: at least three of them destroy themselves, probably because they cannot bear their guilt.

Others who betray are similarly punished. Regis Sheffield reveals his treason near the end—a short while later he is lying in the crater made by PyrE, "drawn and quartered" (chapter 15)—an old punishment, but still effective.

Sam Quatt plays nursemaid to Gully to repay Jiz for some previous desertion, then gets killed as Jiz and Gully flee; he has paid his debt. When, shortly before that, Jiz apologises to Sam for the trouble Gully gave him, the following conversation ensues:

"I had it coming after what I did to you when you were copped out in Memphis" [says Sam].

"Running out on me was only natural, Sam."

"We always do what's natural, only sometimes we shouldn't do it" (chapter 6).

This is one of the lessons Gully must learn: the difference between doing what is "natural" and doing what one "should." He "runs out," betrays, and victimizes almost everyone he meets. This is "natural" to the basic Gully Foyle. His record calls him "The stereotype Common Man," whose "intellectual potential" is "stunted." He is "like some heavily armored creature, sluggish and indifferent" (chapter 1). The early Gully is not far removed from pure animal, something Jiz realizes ever before she has seen his tiger face, an obvious symbol of his brutish character. After he tells her about flinging a bomb at the *Vorga*, Jiz tells him:

"But you were a fool trying to blow up the 'Vorga' like that. You're like a wild beast trying to punish the trap that injured it" (chapter 5).

But Jiz is only one of the three women instrumental in Gully's education, redemption, and transformation into the lamb. The first one he meets, Robin Wednesbury (Wednesday's child is full of woe), serves as both victim of the tiger and teacher to the student. Without doubt, Robin is the most innocent and vulnerable of the three women, the defenseless bird pounced on by the vicious tiger. Gully easily manages to intimidate her with threats of exposing her as an alien-belligerent and, when she displays her fear by screaming and her disgust by telesending (". . .*you filthy, hideous. . .thing.*"—chapter 3), he rapes her. As Geoffrey Fourmyle, he later kidnaps her from a hospital where she had been confined after attempting suicide, because she had lost her job as well as her family; however, she is also obsessed with sex and "the brute who destroyed me" (chapter 8). It seems likely that her rape by Gully has more than a little to do with her suicide attempt. He convinces her to work for him with a combination of subtle threats and bribery (intimations that he can help her find her mother and sisters).

So Robin becomes Gully's guide through the world of high society and his search for the *Vorga* crew. Although she is very often nearly hysterical at his treatment of crew members (e.g., when he "works" on Forrest and then nearly drowns him—chapter 9), she remains with him, distrusting, disgusted, waiting to be victimized again, and sworn to destroy him eventually.

After the bomb attack, Gully returns to St. Pat's to find a Robin who has escaped into near-insanity from her terror at the bombing. He brings her back to reality, not very gently, and berates her for escaping: "First suicide. Now this. What next?" (chapter 11). Then Robin diagnoses Gully's illness: he too runs away, by attacking reality to make it fit his insane pattern. And she tries to buy her freedom from him: he again betrays her, lying to receive the information he wants. At first it seems she will accept the continued servitude, until Gully explains he needs her as "a Romance Secretary. I'm in love with Olivia Presteign." Robin explodes in vindictive fury: calling Olivia *"that white corpse!"* and promising to destroy Gully, she jaunts straight to Y'ang Yeovil of Central Intelligence. Why Gully's passion for Olivia should finally push Robin to rebellion is less than clear. Has she harbored some sort of masochistic attachment to her rapist, so that her explosion is pure jealousy? Does she sense Olivia's true nature? Or is it her job demotion to romance secretary? Whatever the reason, finally the bird has turned on the worm.

Robin betrays Gully who has betrayed her. She, like Gully, seeks revenge. Ironically, her determination leads her to the only person who has ever understood her, the man already in love with her. When Gully meets her in his time-jaunting thirty years later, she has married Y'ang Yeovil and is willing to help him escape from the trap in which he is caught:

> "Why are you helping me. . .after all I've done to you?"
> "That's all forgiven and forgotten, Gully" (chapter 15).

Robin's desire for vengeance, her determination to destroy Gully, leads to her own salvation and redemption—love and mercy for the enemy.

The second woman important to Gully Foyle's redemption is Jisbella McQueen, whose name obviously alludes to the biblical Queen Jezabel, a woman of great strength and power, but also wicked and manipulative. Jisbella's actions in the novel are not particularly wicked (aiding and abetting a criminal is her major crime), but Gully first meets her in Gouffre Martel (literally, the abyss or chasm of torment), a prison for criminal "patients": Jiz is doing time for larceny. Much more than this, we never learn about her background, but her connection with Sam Quatt and Harley Baker's Freak Factory suggests an association with the underworld. The original Jezabel often duped her husband, but Gully is not so manipulable. From their first encounter on the Whisper Line, Jiz takes upon herself the role of teacher ("Got to educate you, man, is all"—chapter 5), but her pupil is less than docile. He drags her with him on a lunatic, unplanned escape despite her protests, apparently plays havoc with attempts at subterfuge while Sam Quatt nursemaids him, again drags Jiz away in the escape from the Freak Factory, and finally deserts her to the authorities, betraying the one friend he had.

But Jisbella's efforts to socialize Gully begin the long, slow process of character shaping. When she meets him in Gouffre Martel, he is little more than pure animal, blindly bent on revenge on the ship that passed him by. It is Jiz who points out the folly of attacking the *Vorga* rather than its commander and begins training him in proper speech as well as thought patterns, "drilling" her own education into him. Even more importantly, Jiz convinces him, through a painfully slow use of rage and repetition, of his weakness, his reliance on brute force rather than on intellect. When they are escaping from prison, an opportunity seized by Gully with little thought but with a confidence in immediate action, they seem to be trapped in a series of endless caverns. Jisbella screams at him, "You pull everything down to your imbecile level and you've pulled me down too. Run. Fight. Punch. That's all you know. Beat. Break. Blast. Destroy—!" (chapter 5).

Her attempts to make him realize the brute level at which he operates continue. Unlike the weak and gentle Robin, Jizbella knows how to fight back and she wars with Gully on his own level. But she has her limits: at first she refuses to pay Baker for anaesthesia for the operation to remove the tattoo ("Let Foyle suffer"—chapter 6) to repay him for the grief he has caused her and Sam Quatt; but later she relents, telling Quatt that she's ashamed of herself for "cruelty to dumb animals." So Gully receives anaesthesia and we learn that Jiz is not the brute Gully is, particularly when we see him later performing unanaesthetized vivisection on a helpless Kempsey. It is also Jiz who suggests to Gully that he is morally responsible for helping the Scientific People repair the damage done to their asteroid (chapter 7), an obligation he does not feel until the very end of the novel, when he follows her advice.

Jisbella's and Gully's relationship is always passionate, a mixture of fury and retaliation that generally ends in sex. By the time they escape the Freak Factory on Sam Quatt's Weekender, Jiz loathes Gully for his desertion of Quatt. They slap each other and she calls him names ("Ghoul. . .Liar. . .Cheat."—chapter 7), but her floating red hair and burning expression change his anger to passion and, with her still accusing him ("Lecher. . .Animal. . . ."), their war is transmuted into love-making.

Robin later becomes Gully's social arbiter, telesending to him at social gatherings what his behavior should be. However, this ploy earlier occurs to Gully during his honeymoon with Jiz on the Weekender. In the calm after their love-making, Gully admits his being driven, his lack of control, and says, "If I could carry you in my pocket, Jiz. . .to warn me. . . stick a pin in me. . . ." Her response perhaps best sums up the lesson that Gully learns and is able to practice by the end of the novel: "Nobody can do it for you, Gully. You have to learn yourself" (chapter 7).

Shortly before he abandons her, Jiz shows him one last thing: that his tiger-mask, surgically erased, reappears in stress:

> "You said you wished you could carry me in your pocket to stick pins in you when you lose control. You've got something better that that, Gully, or worse, poor darling. You've got your face."
> "No!" he said. "No!"
> "You can't ever lose control, Gully. You'll never be able to drink too much, eat too much, love too much, hate too much. . . .You'll have to hold yourself with an iron grip." (chapter 7).

Jisbella's reward for her help is to be deserted: as she pleads with Gully for rescue, he rockets away, "the blood-red stigmata of his possession" flaring on his face. Yet, ironically, his betrayal results in Jisbella's eventual happiness, much as Gully's betrayal of Robin (and hers of him leads to her happiness. Jiz and Saul Dagenham fall in love and, by the time Gully, as Geoffrey Fourmyle, meets her again, Jiz is a redeemed woman. Her hostility toward Gully has disappeared. Although she toys with him, leading him to believe she has revealed all to Dagenham, in fact she has not. Her only revenge is to leave him without explaining what PyrE is.

The one scene we see between Jiz and Saul shows us the depth of tenderness between them: the tough and bitter Jiz has become gentle and loving, more concerned with the stress her lover is under than with plans for revenge. Gully learned much from Jisbella, but Dagenham has clearly learned more from her love, and the most poignant scene in the book occurs as he tells her, "You've changed me completely. I'm a sane man again," and they kiss "through three inches of lead glass" (chapter 12).

Neither Robin or Jisbella can completely reform Gully, although each has a major share in his transformation. Ironically, each is repaid as she meets through her relationship with Gully, a man she can love and trust. Thirty years later, Robin has married, and Jiz is Jiz Dagenham.

Also ironically, the woman who finally pushes Gully into redemption is the one who loves him as he was, the brute. Olivia, the regal and bloodthirsty daughter of Presteign, is the crucial figure of his redemption. Her name might remind us of Livia, a Roman emperor's wife who killed most of her own family. Like Gully with his mask, Olivia shows her deformity: her albino coloring with red eyes, "an exquisite statue of marble and coral" (chapter 3). Also like Gully, Olivia suffers a driving obsession with revenge: in her case, for her "blindness" that allows her to see beauty in bombing raids but prevents her from leading a normal life. The two resemble one another in drive and compulsion so much that it is no wonder they fall in love. The tragic irony, of course, results from their having been unknowing enemies since the beginning.

Presteign exults to Gully as Geoffrey Fourmyle that "We have always had a fatal weakness for blood and money. . . . Without mercy, without forgiveness, without hypocrisy" (chapter 11). He later comments to Olivia that he is glad she has not inherited it. In fact, Olivia makes more famous villains pale by comparison. Although she appears only five times, she is described each time in imagery that emphasizes her hardness, her lack of humanity: a "statue of marble and coral" (Chapter 3); "a Snow Maiden, an Ice Princess with coral eyes and coral lips" with "a husky silvery voice. . .a cool, slim hand" (chapter 11); "a marble statue . . .the statue of exaltation" (chapter 11). Always, she is cold, hard, unyielding. Her appearance and her handicap have isolated her from humanity until she has become a monster (her father's excessive protection of her has no doubt added to the situation). Her statuelike appearance suggests her marble heart; her blindness may be symbolic as well as literal: she simply does not see other people in her own "private life" (chapter 14), as she calls it.

Olivia's and Gully's meeting in the garden reveals their mutually inhuman passions. He starts to rescue Jiz, then Robin, but chooses finally, to look for Olivia. He finds her, ironically, in the garden (Olivia's proper setting would hardly be a background of flowers, so this is January, and she chooses to stand on a marble bench). More appropriately, their courtship takes place while bombs land all around them and Olivia challenges Gully to continue his war for her heart: "Make it a savage war between us. Don't win me. . .destroy me!" (chapter 11).

And so, we assume, he does. It is Gully's later realization of Olivia' monstrousness that triggers his own redemption. Although she begs him to stay with her, arguing that they are a natural pair who share strength and hatred enough to destroy whatever interferes with either of them, he leaves her, saying, "I look through your blind eyes, my love whom loathe, and I see myself. The tiger's gone" (chapter 14). Olivia provides the mirror for Gully Foyle: she is blind, but he sees himself in her, and the horror of that vision recreates the man.

The new Gully born from the inferno of old St. Pat's, where he ha narrowly escaped death by time-jaunting, is a man of conscience and moral awareness far different from the sluggish brute who narrowly escaped death aboard the *Nomad*. He has seen his own monstrous self in Olivia's eyes and he has, through his time-jaunting as the Burning Man, been his own conscience to his former self. The Burning Man has appeared to Gully at crucial moments in his vendetta, each time trying to rescue him or warn him, usually from situations in which the old Gully was inflicting pain on others. Its first appearance was on the beach in Australia after Gully had murdered Forrest in his attempt to pry information out of him (chapter 9). Robin tells him that the figure is himself, "burning in hell," but Gully ignores her. The figure appears twice more in chapter 10, once after Gully has caused Sergei Orel's death and once when Gully has been captured by Y'ang Yeovil's men (this appearance seems to be purely for Gully's own escape). Later, the Burning Man peers through a porthole of the ship on which Gully is vivisecting Kempsey. Gully misinterprets its presence as "a sign, a good luck sign. . .a Guardian Angel. . .," encouraging him to continue his bloody investigation. The Burning Man's last appearance is in chapter 13 when Gully is questioning Lindsey Joyse; it tells him of her pain and Olivia's perfidy. In chapter 15, we are with Gully, who is the Burning Man, aflame with the pangs of conscience and the physical, real flames of the PyrE explosion: as he jaunts back into the past, his agony increases with each stop along the way. All people who repent must suffer pangs of remorse, but Gully, thanks to Bester's use of this special form of time-travel, must re-experience this pain in its original form. The Burning Man becomes a symbol of Gully's soul which must suffer and almost die to be redeemed.

Fittingly, in the last chapter, as Gully tries to decide what to do with PyrE, the "stigmata" reappear on his face, and he says, "I want to get rid of this damnable cross I'm carrying. . . ." Gully has endured his crucifixion and the tiger has been resurrected as a lamb.

Part of Gully's social retribution is the disposal of PyrE: those offering him suggestions and orders in the last chapter discover the lamb still has a bit of claw and fang. Gully may have gained a conscience, but he has not lost his strength. Presteign offers him power and Olivia; Dagenham offers glory; Jisbella wants him to destroy the secret. In a neatly executed intellectual rebuttal, Gully turns the table and brings consternation upon all when he points out that their desires are not so simple, that each course of action suggested, if perfectly carried through, would result in great pain (a line of logic that the old Gully, who saw things in black or white only, never would have comprehended, much less been able to construct). Each of them, says Gully, is "nothing but response. . .mechanical reaction in prescribed grooves." Ironically, it is Presteign's bartender robot (who fits literally, not metaphorically, Gully's description) who points the way: the people in the room, who supposedly have free will, cannot see beyond their own compulsions. The robot has been disrupted by Dagenham's radiation and suggests the fairest solution: "A man is a member of society first, and an individual second. You must go along with society, whether it chooses destruction or not." And, if society is stupid and confused, "You must teach society," it tells Gully. The driven, compulsive man must lead, for life must be lived even if life itself may be a freak for which no reason can be found (chapter 16).

In this scene, Gully accepts his role—the leader, driven, but capable of showing the rest of the world a direction. He distributes the PyrE around in the world in the next scene, despite attempts to stop him. It is time the common people take responsibility for themselves; he tells Presteign, Dagenham, and Y'ang Yeovil. "I was one of them before I turned tiger. They can all turn uncommon if they're kicked awake like I was." Then he turns to the people and tells them, "Die or live and be great." Appropriately, he delivers this challenge from a statue of Eros, god of love. For Gully, in his mad race around the world, scattering PyrE to the ignorant masses, demonstrates his trust in, and love for, those masses: because he has come from them, he knows both what they are and what they have the potential for becoming.

Gully, like Gulliver in his travels, has come a long way, and much has happened as a result of his shipwreck. Unlike the original Gulliver, who spends his last days in a stable because he cannot bear his fellow human beings, Gully places his last bet on the Yahoos. He has awakened to a mystical fate—as possible savior of the world. In this process, he has become his own foil: the brutish, selfish lout has become the intelligent and active moral leader.

> Did he who make the Lamb make thee?

> Tiger! Tiger! burning bright
> In the forests of the night.

The lamb resides within the tiger and will be born from him.

The closing scene shows rather obviously what has been strongly suggested before: Gully as a Christ/savior figure. After space-jaunting among the heavens, Gully returns to "the womb of his birth" (chapter

35

16), aboard the asteroid of the Scientific Peoples (thus doing what Jisbella has asked him to long before: making restitution to the people whose home he savaged). The elements of this last part remind us of the birth and life of Christ: Joseph and Moira (very similar to "Mary"), who sinks to her knees when she finds Gully curled in a "tight foetal ball;" the "holy of holies" where Joseph, a priest resides; the silver tray and water with which Moira washes Gully. Joseph knows that he is merely asleep, that Gully has already punished himself, and so the two sit down "alongside the world. . .prepared to await the awakening." Gully descended to hell in the flames of old St. Pat's, and now he shall arise—as what, we do not know, but we can suspect from the consistent imagery of this last section, that he will awaken as a major force and shaper of human destiny, a messiah to usher in a new age.

V.

THE COMPUTER CONNECTION

The Computer Connection is probably the most unconnected work of fiction Bester has ever done. The novel's title was an obvious attempt to capitalize on the popularity of the blockbuster movie, *The French Connection* (the work had been serialized in *Analog* as *The Indian Giver* and published in England as *Extro*, either one a more apt title than *The Computer Connection*). It received mixed reviews: although reviewers were clearly excited about Bester's first novel in twenty years, most felt it was seriously flawed. Most found it readable for its constant surprises (typical of Bester), but criticized its lack of originality (the mad computer plot, even then, had been done, re-done, and over-done) and narrative logic. As Baird Searles (*The Science Fiction Review*, May 1975) put it, "If you need a prop, *deus* it out of the *machina* with little or no explanation—just keep the wheels going, man." George Warren (*Science Fiction Review*, February 1976) seemed to be the most disappointed and blamed what he felt was its lack of readability on Bester's having lost his voice, a tragedy resulting in a "ghastly, cutesy-wutesy style" and "trendy-kid-writer stuff." Several reviewers attempted to apologize for it. Robert Silverberg (*Odyssey*, Spring 1976) argued that "Bester's third-best novel is superior to almost everyone else's best-best," and Frederick Patten (*Delap's*, July 1975) called it "extremely good instead of superb."

Certainly the novel is disjointed; although Bester's previous works had all been subject to mild accusations of this, this novel pushes disjointedness into near chaos. Characters appear and disappear (and sometimes reappear) with kaleidoscopic irregularity, the plot quite regularly sidetracks itself, incidents and basic premises go unexplained, and even the language is at times hard to follow. Earlier works suggest Bester's fertile imagination can easily provide more than enough ideas for a single book; *The Computer Connection* contains enough material for a dozen other novels. It is a manic attack on practically everything while the plot and characters are almost buried underneath. What plot there is involves a group of immortals, one of whom has become linked to a computer; as a result he is intent upon the take-over of the world by a group of "cryonauts," three pilots who return as foetuses from the test run using cryonics. They survive, growing into what the deranged hero believes might be the replacements for the human race, a more peaceful form of man. In *The Computer Connection*'s insanely fragmented construction of a fictional world, it resembles some mainstream literature unusual in science fiction. Bester's novel, however, might bear comparison, for instance, with some of Thomas Pynchon's works. Pynchon and Bester both share a suspicion of a crazy world where conspiracy abounds (with or without paranoia) and characters bounce energetically from one mad scene to the the next. Ben Reich (*TDM*) and Gully Foyle (*TSMD*) live in worlds unlike ours but still recognizable; Edward Curzon's world bears little resemblance to ours—it is a world gone insane, along with its inhabitants. Pynchon's vision is much bleaker and baser than Bester's (the black humorist versus the clown), but Bester's Sequoya Guess and Fee-5 Grauman's Chinese would fit right into the world inhabited by Pynchon's Oedipa Maas and Brigadier Pudding. In this, *The Computer Connection* may be Bester's noblest attempt—not a success but a fascinating failure.

Almost every possible science-fiction topic and gimmick utilized at the time the novel was written has been worked into *The Computer Connection*. The novel may well be, in part, a game—how many familiar patterns can be jammed into one short novel? Since Bester is on record as saying that he abhors the clichés of science fiction, one way of approaching the novel is to see it as a parody. Thus we have immortality (the Group); time travel (chapter 1: the first sidetrack in the novel as the narrator is sent back in time to Thomas Chatterton's era); computers (better yet, a mad computer, out to destroy the human race); space travel (Curzon and Natoma go to Ceres in chapter 9); space colonization (Hic Haec Hoc is located and brought back from Titan, a colony with intriguing characteristics in chapter 9); aliens (Twinkles, in chapter 13); evolved man (the cryonauts in chapter 12); speculation on future society (nearly every page); cloning (chapter 15); a mad scientist (Sequoya Guess); matter transportation (people can "project" themselves other places and several do so in the course of the novel); transplants (Captain Nemo's Laura in chapter 2); cryonics/cryogenics; and numerous others. None is fully developed, and several are not even germane to the plot (the time travel, for instance). Yet all are jammed in, suggesting a possible satiric comment on the methods of science fiction ("if one gimmick is good, let's try 'em all"). Unfortunately, although wit is expended on many of these separate areas, each is too briefly depicted to provide much impact. Although this sort of thing may sound like a clever premise in the abstract, in actuality, it may only frustrate most readers. Or, as Gerald Jonas (*New York Times*, July 20, 1975) commented in his review, "The trouble with books like 'The Computer Connection' is that they cannot possibly be as much fun to read as they obviously are to write." The book fairly explodes with ideas shooting off in all directions. Unhappily, they too often explode harmlessly before they have developed enough to do any damage to the target.

If the novel is an attempted parody of science-fiction conventions and clichés, it is far less successful than another, shorter parody that was written about the same time: "Here Come the Clones," subtitled "A Complete Short History of SF Writing With Fifty All-Purpose Footnotes." Since the purpose here is clearly to satirize, the supposed plot that makes little sense is not bothersome, and the appended footnotes provide the core material, pointing out the hackneyed ideas and mistakes all too typical of much of science fiction. And, since the piece is short less than three pages), it sustains itself until the end.

As is typical with Bester, the world his characters inhabit in *The Computer Connection* is extrapolation of our own, pushed further than those described in his earlier works. In this case, much of the extrapolation comes directly from the events of the late 1960's and often seems dated by now (student protests, for example). But numerous areas are attacked with typical scattergun technique: politics and corporations, social prost, education and language, mass entertainment and advertising, and minority (and majority) groups.

And, most of the fun of the novel is its portrayal of society. Plot and characters remain sketchy to the last. The most charming character, Fee-5, is unhappily killed off little more than halfway through. Since she has been introduced as one of the major characters and certainly one of the more likeable, her loss is deeply felt—but more by the reader than the characters, who make little fuss about her death until the end when we find that she may be cloned from what is left of her corpse. Fee-5 as a precocious adolescent in inexperienced but passionate pursuit of the man she loves is far more credible than the other, adult characters.

Sequoya Guess, as antihero, is more or less a standard mad scientist (although an American Indian), obsessed with his plot to substitute his cryos for the "plague of man." Fortunately, but untraditionally (and more than a little unbelievably), he can be saved, and, at the end of the novel, he must mature all over again, into a better person we assume (somewhat like Ben Reich's fate in *TDM*). His cryos are left to run Extro, the massive super-computer; Curzon, the narrator (and hero who pursues Sequoya, much like Lincoln Powell's role in *TDM*), trusts them to do right (an assumption based on very little except his perception of their apparently gentle natures), so the mad scientist does succeed in a small way.

Edward Curzon/Grand Guignol (called "Guig," whose pronunciation is a complete puzzle) tells his own story. This first person narration may be another major flaw of the novel as there seems little reason for it. We seldom go into Curzon's mind to know, really, what sort of a person he is. We know he is immortal, a bit crazy (as evidenced by his attempts to kill people to give them immortality—he has yet to succeed as the novel opens and he has lost count of his attempts), energetic (but then, all the characters are), and we are told he is envied by the Group for his passion (chapter 12), but we see little evidence for it. His caring for humanity could be better demonstrated than by his assassination attempts: these, and his sudden infatuation with Natoma, make him seem more adolescent than Fee-5, his ward. The love story of Curzon and Natoma provides yet another incredible aspect of the plot. They are total strangers from totally different cultures who cannot even communicate and who are linked in marriage sheerly by accident; yet after their wedding night, Curzon exults, "Now I was in love for the first time, it seemed, and it made me love and understand the whole damn lunatic world" (chapter 5). It is beautifully romantic, but adolescent, particularly for a man who is on the far side of 200 years old.

However, we are expected to accept this, as the novel ends with a neatly structured nuclear family: the lovely Natoma, dedicated to husband and brother (everything but feminism has been extrapolated, it seems), her loving husband who has become an adopted Indian son, and their fictive son, Sequoya, whom they must help grow up. And they are expecting a daughter, the cloned Fee-5.

Perhaps all of them will grow up—or perhaps the theme of the novel is that, in a lunatic world, no one can grow up, for sane maturity is impossible.

While interesting for its partial extrapolation of society and its hints at character, *The Computer Connection* is Bester's weakest novel. It embodies his worst flaws as a writer and, as such, it probably is most interesting as a study of excessive style. Those techniques which worked before in *TDM* and *TSMD*—the rapid scene shifts, the detailed plot, the piling on of image—are here in *The Computer Connection* in excess. Those qualities which made his two earlier novels classics make this novel a failure.

VI.

SHORT STORIES

Bester has not been the most prolific writer of science fiction short stories, but the bulk of these shorter works are well-crafted pieces that have seldom been discussed at any length. With the exception of most of his earliest stories, all are still available, having been reprinted in collections (see the annotated bibliography). Those qualities that have made TDM and TSMD classics appear in the short stories: the wit and satire, the oddball characters compelled by their own powerfully idiosyncratic drives, the fast-paced action, the literal and metaphorical sparks, and the flames of energy and enthusiasm.

An informal poll taken by Ed Ferman for a retrospective issue of Fantasy and Science Fiction (October 1979) asked contributors of long standing and lifetime subscribers to list favorite stories and writers. "Fondly Fahrenheit," Bester's strongest and most popular story, was reprinted in the issue. And the poll respondents gave the large majority of their votes to Alfred Bester as their favorite writer. Respondents were not asked to give reasons for their selections, but since Theodore Sturgeon trailed Bester as a "distant second," we might speculate that these two authors are both highly regarded because they share an overriding concern with the people in their fiction. Both deal with the eccentric, lonely character who does not quite belong. Sturgeon perhaps shows more compassion for these misfits, but Bester views them with more excitement and humor.

To read Bester's stories in chronological order is to watch the growth of a writer, at first reproducing the plots and ideas of his contemporaries in the pulps to a groping for his own themes and ideas, and, finally, a discovery of his own unique voice, polished, urbane, and witty.

Ten of Bester's first fourteen stories have not been reprinted and can be found only in the aging pulp magazines that first printed them—and they are probably best left there. With only a very few exceptions, they give little hint of the stories to come. The mature Bester favors the compulsive character: the younger Bester was enamoured of the mad scientist, who constructs a machine (in his university laboratory or basement workshop) that almost results in destruction of the scientist or his world or that provides a means of enslaving the world (from which diabolical plot the clever young hero must rescue everyone). Little attention is paid to character development in these stories—the people have names and occupations but remain mere puppets, moving the plot along to a happy ending (destruction of the machine, usually by way of the obligatory fistfight and chemical explosion near the end). The technique is nondescript pulp style, with summary of action used as often as dramatic detail and the two most common emphatic words being "incredible" and "incredibly." And the heroes can sound embarassingly self-righteous about their world-saving endeavors, like the intern who has saved the world from a ray that turns people into deformed monstrosities, when he throws away his gun at the end and says smugly, "Thank god, I've no more use for that. I'm a doctor—not a destroyer" ("Slaves of the Life Ray").

The stories also frequently reflect the era they were written in. In "Life for Sale," another diabolical-plot-to-rule-the-world-by-machine story, the subplot deals with "suffragettes" who want the vote in the future city and provide a strip show as diversion for the mob gathered outside the building they want to seize. By the end, the male hero has, as usual, saved the world, and he and the suffragette leader have fallen in love (although she had been irked earlier when he had kissed her, because he knew she was dating someone else). She apologizes for having been so foolish (for having wanted the vote and being ready to fight for it, we assume), and they kiss while the hero's sidekick edges toward a beautiful blonde. The portrayal of women as the inferior sex would not have raised an eyebrow in 1942, but it would raise tempers now. "The Probable Man," a time travel-alternate world story, has its hero fighting off the descendants of the Nazis in an alternate world where his allies are called "Readers" and are the descendants of the educated. Perhaps an intruiguing, relevant tale in 1941, it seems simplistic today. (However, the contemporary reader may be struck by the references to the Readers using Uranium 235 to light their tunnel hideaways and to the war's ending in 1945 in the hero's own time track.)

But the Bester humor does occasionally surface in these early attempts; although not the honed wit of his mature works, it does glimmer through the stories whose major charm is now nostalgic and historical. In "The Biped, Reegan," the last stages of a human being-ant war are narrated by an ant who reports to his "Imperial Maternity" on the anatomy of male and female human beings. "The bipeds discerned differences in sex by vision," he tells her, and then confidently concludes that people are "the ugliest life-form our earth has produced." The ant's eye-view provides a bit of humor to an otherwise clichéd story. In "The Pet Nebula," a professor implausibly creates a tiny nebula that keeps growing and is seemingly impervious to all attacks. The little nebula takes the form of a seahorse and seems almost lovable as it meanders from street light to street light, "looking for a friend." And the ending almost redeems the absurd plot when, after the nebula has been destroyed, the narrator tells his friend, tongue-in-cheek, that at least the episode had succeeded in rousting him out of bed. It helps to know that the characters do not take the plot seriously, either.

Too often, though, the attempted wit falls flat as plot is sacrificed for too obvious irony and puns. In "Voyage to Nowhere," three criminals on Jupiter plan an escape (whose methods, especially a trek through a sewer system, seem remarkably similar to Gully Foyle's later escape from Gouffre Martel in *TSMD*) so they won't be deported to their native lanets of Venus, Mercury, and Mars where they would each face the orrible punishment of their legal systems (suffocation, garroting, olitary confinement). But each man meets his end in precisely the way is home planet would have dictated, and, after the first death, the plot is ll too predictable (and all too tortuous, as the improbable follows the npossible so that the destiny of each can be met). Touches like atospheric jets of oxygen on Titan that result in speeded-up lives of the nimals around them fascinate, but remain unintegrated into the plot.

A similar situation occurs in "The Push of a Finger," which offers ice touches like a society stabilized by its insistence on balanced opposg forces (*e.g.*, each newspaper is paired with another newspaper that as the opposing point of view). But the whole, complicated plot rests on shaggy dog pun—that a line spoken by the narrator at the end can be ritten as an equation. This pun, we are told, will dictate the end of the orld. This conclusion makes the whole story seem a self-parody; hether intentional or not, it is hard to say.

One early story comes closer to Bester's later satiric mode and his ocasional attitude over the years toward science fiction as one of the lesser orms of literature. The narrator of "The Unseen Blushers", a pulp writer, neets a stranger at a luncheon (the setting and characters are clearly based n the lunches Bester attended with other science fiction pulp writers in the arly 1940's). The visitor tells the story of a twenty-third century time traveler who comes to find out about a writer considered, three hundred years ater, the Shakespeare of his time. The researcher finds only a poorly-urnished apartment with its genius tenant, "a dull, undistinguished peron thrashing about on the bed" and a striking scarcity of manuscripts. The researcher will have to return to his own time without the material eeded to finish his doctorate. But the narrator believes the tale he has eard—only that morning he had found a piece of paper dated 2241 in is apartment. The ending is probably too obvious (a tendency Bester ater curbed, preferring ambiguity), but the basic theme has merit: the crowd-pleasers of today may well provide material for the academics of omorrow (a direction academic criticism has already begun to take).

Two other early stories also stand out from the rest: while offering less than the later, more crafted stories, they move away from the clichés of the 1940's and offer promise of later work. "Adam and No Eve" is an admitted attempt to rework the clichéd last-man-and-last-woman-left-on-earth-after-cataclysm story. Bester remarked about the inception of the story, "I'd just about had it with the Adam and Eve device in science fiction" (*STL*). Although it retains the tried-and-true plot of the lone inventor in his basement building a dangerous rocketship, in this case the diabolical machine really does destroy the world, and there is no clever young hero to prevent it. Stephen Krane (whose name might remind us of Stephen Crane's Henry Fleming, a young sacrificial victim) turns the earth into a ball of ashes with his rocket exhaust (the science involved is dubious at best), but he returns and undertakes an arduous crawl to the sea, realizing that the chemicals in his body will begin life again. While the story offers a twist on the standard plot, even Bester now calls it "rather jejune" (*STL*). Certainly it is melodramatic, and the plot does not quite cohere: Krane's dog goes along on the rocket, returns to earth with him, and has to be killed when it attacks him. Bester now says he does not know why the dog had to be incinerated (*STL*); actually, it is a mystery why the dog was in the story to begin with. There is also a strange lack of guilt on Krane's part: although he does give his body to reseed life, his responsibility for the destruction of an entire planet does not seem to bother him very much. There is also a disconcerting change in point of view in the last paragraph. Nevertheless, the story is one of Bester's strongest for that time and is considered by many as a classic. (As such, it was in good company when it was first published in *Astounding* in September, 1941: its companions were Asimov's "Nightfall" and the last part of Heinlein's "Methusaleh's Children.")

"Hell is Forever" is a strange mixture of social and moral comment, existentialism, and the occult. Six socialites of the future hole up in Lady Sutton's castle dungeon-bomb shelter. They proudly think of themselves as the "Six Decadents" who try to overcome their sated spirits with ever weirder pranks (with obvious thanks to Huysmans. This type of society appears later in *TSMD*). As the result of one of their practical jokes to scare Lady Sutton, a real demon appears and offers each of the five remaining (Lady Sutton has apparently been literally scared to death) "his own heart's desire." The rest of the story is an exploration of each character's fantasy fulfilled. Like the characters in "Voyage to Nowhere," each one receives what he/she deserves. The immoral artist discovers that, as a god, he can create only in his own image, so his creations are deformed monstrosities. The selfish wife who wishes to be free of her husband realizes that by killing him, she kills the better part of herself and must live forever with only her own depraved lusts as companion. The husband tries to commit suicide but only condemns himself to eternal agony. The beautiful temptress who has never known what she really wanted because she never understood herself becomes the victim of a primitive people and their god. The liveliest section is the writer's fantasy, which is to know the truth. He finds himself in a hell that is straight out of animated fairy tales. Satan's "central administrators" are cute dwarfs whose spells succeed only in putting one of their number asleep. Satan turns out to be an old man who controls all with a huge adding machine that is in reality a marionettes' crossbar (Rice's *The Adding Machine* was probably one of the literary influences here). The writer asks that the string to earth be cut, but Satan says that he cannot and promptly falls asleep. "Truth is hell," concludes the writer. "We're puppets." But his bitterness is interrupted when, at the end of the episode, he suddenly sees a silver thread connected to Satan's own neck. The writer responds by laughing genuinely, for the first time in his life, at "the blessedly unkowable cosmos." The suggestion seems to be that we are better off not being able to understand the workings of the universe. This pisode is worth the story as a whole for its humor and its vivid depiction of an omnipotent being.

The story ends on a rather pedestrian note: Lady Sutton was not really dead, only faking. She is really the ancient goddess, Astaroth, playing a joke on five people who had been killed by a bomb before they arrived at her home. She did it because she was bored and concludes that "there's no hell like the hell of boredom" and that "each living creature creates its own hell evermore." Bester has said that, although he cannot remember writing the story, he can see the literary influences of what he was reading at the time, and the story does, in its occasional pretentiousness (Latin phrasing, for example) and allusions, sound like a young writer seeking his own voice. Even more striking, however, is the strong similarity, in theme and plot, to Sartre's mainstream classic, *No Exit*, written four years after "Hell is Forever" (1941).

The voice of that young writer rings loudly and clearly in the later stories. There was an eight-year gap between "Hell is Forever" and the next story, "Oddy and Id" (1950, published as "The Devil's Invention"). Those eight years were filled with writing for radio and television, and skills were developed. The return to science fiction is explained by Bester:

> I went back to science fiction to keep my cool. It was a safety valve, an escape hatch, therapy for me. The ideas which no show would touch could be written as science fiction stories and I could have the satisfaction of seeing them come to life ("My Affair with Science Fiction").

From 1950 on, the stories came slowly but fairly regularly. These later works are, even at their worst (and there are a few clinkers), good reading and, at their best, provocative and original. If there is a major theme, it is that of the folly of wishing to be something other than what we are, someplace other than where we are, some time other than when we are. Escape to another time or even to a fantasy of our own devising will not usually work. Here and now is best.

Most commonly, fantasy and time travel appear as the methods of unsuccessful escape. Time travel has been a standard device since H. G. Wells, and Bester's stories most often focus, not on the travel itself but, like Wells, purely as method to get somewhere else and make a point. Even "The Men Who Murdered Mohammed," a story Bester says "was written solely for the sake of doing an amusing aspect of time travel itself" (*STL*), seems a comment on the futility of time travel as a solution to personal problems. Its protagonist (one of Bester's favorite types, the eccentric oddball) is a genius professor of Applied Compulsion at Unknown University which has a "faculty of some two hundred eccentrics, and a student body of two thousand misfits." He discovers his wife in the arms of another man and, with the logical illogic of many of Bester's lovable eccentrics, Henry Hassel builds a time machine on the spot (he's so brilliant he can build it while the two culprits are still embracing) and tries to change first his wife's past and then the historical past. But each attempt fails, and he keeps returning to the present to find Mrs. Hassel still in her lover's arms. Finally he learns that "time is a private matter," that an individual can destroy only his own past and, thus, his own self. By the end, Hassel is a ghost. Although the plot may have the potential for tragedy, the whimsicality of the central character prevents it, so the tale is a humorous one, ending happily as the apparently undistressed ghost goes merrily off to hear a lecture, forgetting his unfaithful wife and his spectral state. The story points out the laughable peculiarities of genius, that species not quite in touch with reality, not really sharing the concerns of us non-geniuses. And Bester's mad scientist here is a far more enjoyable and original creation than those who appeared in his earlier stories.

Time travel cannot solve one's problems; knowledge of the future via time travel will not help, either. Oliver Wilson Knight, in "Of Time and Third Avenue," accidently picks up an almanac of the future that has somehow slipped back into the past. A traveler from the almanac's time convinces Knight that knowledge of the future might bring him success but not happiness because he would be "cheating" by not using his own ability to succeed. "Through all your pointless life you will wish you had played honestly the game of life." Knight finally agrees and surrenders the book. The story comes down solidly on the side of individual enterprise and hard work for achievement, rather than any shortcuts to fame and fortune.

One of Bester's finest and most fascinating stories combines time travel with fantasy, suggesting the folly of both. "Hobson's Choice" was based on a satiric sketch, "I remember Hiroshima," Bester wrote for the Paul Winchell Television show ("Epilogue: My Private World of Science Fiction"). Addyer (an appropriate name choice), a dull little statistician, lives in a future world torn by war. The landscape would be bleak were it not for the light satiric touches: for instance, an entire county has been wiped out, "owing to one of those military mistakes of an excessive nature." Addyer's boss (fittingly, Mr. Grande) entertains himself between Addyer's reports by computing how many "bored respirations" he has left in life or trying to integrate "his pulse-rate with his eye-blink." Addyer, another eccentric, fantasizes about living in another era. When he discovers the existence of a time machine and finds that he is to be sent off to another time, he is at first excited. But, as in "Of Time and Third Avenue," the man from the future who runs the machine tries to convince him that, in fact, one is suited only to one's own time. The past offers discomfort and disease; the future, confusion. Language would be a barrier at the other end. Travel to the past with knowledge of the future? "What superior knowledge? Your hazy recollection of science and invention? Don't be a damned fool, Addyer. You enjoy your technology without the faintest idea of how it works," argues the time traveler. And even if Addyer did understand, for instance, radio, he would first need to invent all "the hundred allied technical discoveries that went into it." Addyer's initial confidence is shaken, but he does finally choose an era and disappears "from his time forever." We are not told where he goes, but the title of the story tells us it makes little difference. Thomas Hobson, a liveryman of sixteenth-century England, rented horses strictly in accordance with their position near the door. So a "Hobson's choice" is a lack of choice. Whatever age Addyer chooses, it will be the wrong one. "Half the panhandlers you meet are probably time-bums stuck in the wrong century," says the man from the future. Addyer will undoubtedly be another one. Interspersed with plot action, in chorus fashion, are italicized lines, repeating in a variety of forms of fractured English, a request for the price of a cup of coffee. "Hobson's Choice" ends with a request and explanation from the speaker, a "starveling Japanese transient" who wants to go back home to Hiroshima, 1945. The repeated requests add both humor with their garbled language and a poignancy to Addyer's time fantasies as we realize we cannot live comfortable anywhere but our own time, that "to-day, bitter or sweet, anxious or calm, is the only day for us."

The time traveler appears in more destructive guise in "The Roller Coaster," narrated by David, a man intent upon terrorizing a "hooker" at the opening. David has traveled to our era from the future, and, as he seeks his next victim, we learn that the future he comes from is a time of great passivity whose inhabitants come to our overwrought time, seeing it as an amusement park where they can enjoy our screams of pain. The rising crime rate results from these tourists who "stick pins in us until we blow our tops and give their glands a roller coaster ride." Although time travel may be healthy for those from the future, it offers nothing but pain to us.

More light-heartedly, "The Flowered Thundermug" has its two protagonists catapulted from the fifties into the future by vast explosions. A war has intervened, and American culture has rebuilt on material from Hollywood. America is now Great L. A., all citizens have the names of film stars of the 1930's and 1940's, and their life styles reflect what was projected on the movie screen. The idea is amusing, but it palls after a few pages of madcap action and numerous in-jokes about movies and their stars.

Much more successful and memorable is "Disappearing Act" where shock victims of the War for the American Dream keep vanishing from their hospital ward. The harassed military send for expert after expert, but, although they fight for the American Dream of "Music and Art and Poetry and Culture," they know little about any of these categories (when one victim seems connected to a Diamond Jim Brady, the military brass sends for a lapidary). In an era of supertechnical specialization, the humanities and the human have been forgotten. Finally an historian is released from prison. "In this benighted nation of experts, I'm the last singing grasshopper in the ant heap," he tells the General, who sends for an entomologist to explain the reference. The historian discovers that the shock victims are escaping from a war-filled world into a past created by their own imaginations. Although their refuges are filled with inconsistencies and anachronisms, they have somehow "discovered how to turn dreams into reality," a way to convert imagination into actuality. The generals want to know how to do this, but the historian says only a poet would know. The general orders a poet to be sent to him, but there is none, and this is the "final, fatal disappearance." Clearly a satire on the military mind and excessive reliance on specialization, the story is one of Bester's only works that sees escape from reality as viable. The device used is a reworking of the standard time travel, but the story argues for the power of the human imagination to turn fantasies, no matter how illogical, into reality. As such, it is a story about the artist who creates reality by the sheer power of imagination.

"Time is the Traitor" also offers comment on the individual's perception of time and his fantasies about it. But John Strapp's dreams do not come true. A slight, clerklike man who makes millions by making reliable decisions, he is obsessed with his search for another woman exactly like the fiancée he lost ten years before. His closest friend takes pity on him and manages to have the dead girl cloned, physically and psychically, from her remains. But Strapp rejects her: ten years have changed him and the girl he remembers is not the girl who really was and is. "We only remember the past; we never know it when we meet it." We cannot even return to our own personal past because our fantasies about it would prevent us from recognizing the reality.

Many of Bester's characters are driven by their fantasies, like John Strapp. This makes them at times creatures of freak shows (Gully Foyle of *TSMD*, for instance), but those freaks are, after all, only an exaggeration of the "average" and "normal" among the rest of us. And a large part of the fascination and excitement of Bester's works springs from these driven creatures who, more often than not, are compelled by internal forces they themselves do not understand. But the end result in Bester's fiction is that action grows out of character, rather than action being forced upon character.

In the introduction to "Oddy and Id" (*STL*), Bester explains how his works began to show this concern for psychic compulsion. As a mystery writer for the popular media, he did much research, looking for gimmicks for use as clues in the story. "Eventually I got onto psychiatry and discovered the field was rich in behavior gimmicks. . . . It was a result of this purely pragmatic research that I became hooked on psychiatry and started writing about compulsives and their corrosive effects." It is from this point onward, with the publication of "Oddy and Id" in 1950, that we see the Bester who turned out the classics of science fiction.

Many characters try to escape reality by using time (either travel or fantasizing about it). But others suffer "corrosive effects" because of their own private fantasies. The shell-shocked victims of "Disappearing Act" may be able to live in their dreams, but this leads only to destruction in other stories. At worst, the world suffers; at best, the protagonist

48

ealizes that maturity and creative ability will come only with rejection of his fantasies. In "Oddy and Id," Odysseus Gaul has been born with a rare talent—luck. Events always occur in such a way that their results will benefit him. When this is discovered by his college professors, they decide to teach him and shape him so that he will be a force for good, consciously using his luck for the benefit of mankind. Oddy, a good-natured young man, agrees wholeheartedly: "If I'm an angel. . .then I'll spread heaven around me as far as I can reach." Almost immediately, disasters strike, and Oddy becomes dictator of a universe that "suffers misgovernment, oppression, poverty, and confusion with a cheerful joy that sings nothing but Hosannahs to the glory of Oddy Gaul." At the end of the story, before his professors sink into the insanity of total adoration of the tyrant, they realize that Oddy cannot have concious control over his powers. Each person has a deeply buried id that knows no morality and wants only self-satisfaction, but only Oddy's self has the power to guarantee fulfillment of these desires, and there is no way he, or anyone else, can control the outcome. The best conscious intentions have no effect on the id's desires.

Stuart Buchanan ("Star Light, Star Bright") has another unusual talent. The principal of his school, after reading Stuart's essay about his friends who have super powers and intellects, looks for him. But the search is long and arduous since all evidence of Stuart and his family is missing. Eventually Stuart is located, but the principal finds himself on "a straight white road cleaving infinitely through blackness, stretching onward and onward forever. . . ." The young genius has a talent as strange as Oddy Gaul's: his talent, which he is as unaware of as the young Oddy, is for wishing. When he wishes away people who want to disturb his child's games, they go a long way away. Oddy has no control over his powers, and Stuart is too young to even know he has his, so he is as yet unable to choose what he will do with them.

On the other hand, Jeffrey Halsyon, the protagonist of "5,271,009," does have a choice. He, too, has fantasies (actually, those quite common to most people), but he does not have the power to make them come true, and he must learn to surrender them for his sanity and his work as an artist. This story, according to Bester, was written to accompany a cover illustration of a convict chained to an asteroid with 5,271,009 on his chest. Although stories tailored for illustrations impose often insurmountable barriers to writing a story, in this case, Bester's fertile imagination won out: the result is one of his strangest, yet most memorable, works. Bester says that he was spoofing clichés, people he know, and even himself in this story (STL). In Solon Aquila (a loose Latin translation would give us "lone eagle," although Solon also calls to mind the wise and revered lawmaker of ancient Greece), Bester has given us one of his most vivid characters. In his energy, his mixed personalities, and his capabilities, he is similar to Gully Foyle/Geoffrey Fourmyle of TSMD. Aquila has visited many times and places, as indicated by the linguistic salad he speaks. He is also a connoisseur, a psychiatrist, and more than a bit

Satanic, using his skills to cure the demented Halsyon. He reveals to Ha
syon that, in fact, he is a bad person whose home cannot tolerate hi
and pays him to stay in exile. Ironically, Halsyon's insanity (triggered
a glimpse of Aquila's unguarded expression) is cured by this "bad
Satanic character. Aquila's methods remind us of the earlier demon
"Hell is Forever," but the characters in that story had no choice on
their fantasies were made real by the demon. Halsyon is made to live o
all his adolescent fantasies. The last man on earth learns that wom
despise him because they have no choice but to make love to him. T
falsely condemned prisoner who holds the secret for saving the univer
learns his knowledge is not unique (the crucial secret is that "3 com
after 2, not before"). The child with the knowledge of his adult s
discovers adults do not listen to children (time travel fails again). T
character in a literary classic (a witty parody of *Hamlet*) finally decide
"I'd rather be in a world of my own making:" the illusion of being
character in someone else's creation, with no free will of one's own a
no responsibility, fails. And, finally, the last man on earth meets the la
woman but blows his brains out when she admits she cannot cure h
toothache. "A man cannot start making adult decisions until he h
purged himself of the dreams of his childhood. God dam. Such fantasie
They must go," Aquila tells Halsyon. Art comes from adult fantasie
not the clichéd fantasies of youth. The story ends with our not knowir
what decision Halsyon will make, but we know which choice is the cc
rect one.

The satiric element is strong in "5,271,009" as Bester makes fun
our most common daydreams and of literature as well (Aquila is
parody of Milton's Satan and all his relations ever since, in mainstrea
and science fiction literature). A handful of his stories are pure satir
"MS Found in a Bottle" chortles with glee at the hackneyed plot
mechanical revolution, but the narrator is a member of the upper cla
(preserved for mechanical posterity in the Bronx Zoo) who is given ho
when he sees a rat in a tiara run across the floor of his cage. His fir
thought is the tackiness of a tiara in daytime, but then the rat winks
him, as if to signal yet another revolution. Absurdity runs strong in th
slight, but amusing tale, as a milking machine rapes a farmer's wife, a
Christmas tree lights "get" a young heir preparing a holiday treat for h
nanny. "Travel Diary" is also a facile but amusing satire on high societ
No matter where the bored socialites of the future visit, they seek th
same life style they enjoy at home. The diarist comments at the end tha
"The universe is a great place to visit, but I'd sure hate to live there."
fact, she has only repeated the same activities on all worlds—she has n
really "visited" at all.

"Will You Wait?" blends traditional occultism with twentieth-centu
bureaucracy and suggests that the devil can be found in the yellow pag
(a member of the firm Beelezebub, Belial, Devil and Orgy) and that th
legalities and red tape involved in selling one's soul are so snarled the
days that the would-be victim has to hire the legal firm of Wizar

oodoo, Dowser and Hag to represent him before an arbitration board. The Die-Hard" is an old, old man living in a world changed beyond his cognition. He will not allow his young guardians to "reconstruct" him to a cyborg like themselves; they regard him, rather proudly, as a "Museum of pathology." The story cuts two ways: the new world is ore perfect physically, but it does lack the passion of the old, so we are clined to agree with the old man's last scream, "I'm the last man on rth."

Less graceful, and less skillful are the two weakest of Bester's later ories. "The Animal Fair" offers talking animals and a nauseatingly weet child in what might have been an attempt to parody the literature f anthropomorphic animals, but the plot is contrived and filled with il-gic and inconsistencies. "Out of This World" is narrated by a man ho falls in love with a woman from an alternate world when telephone nes are out of order, so she keeps reaching his office instead of her rlfriend. We finally learn that the Japanese won World War II in her orld, but we do not learn anything more. Whatever poignancy the story ffers is seriously undercut by the narrator's frequent references to feel-ig guilty because he never tells his wife about the phone calls (adding a rring note of domestic conflict) and by his blithe comment at the end aat he is now in love with an ice skater. Domestic conflict, alternate orlds, and poignant love strain against each other, with none taking nematic precedence.

Bester has written better love stories, however. Actually, the mating ame is played more frequently in his stories than in those of his contem-oraries in science fiction. Boys and girls meet, part, and reunite on a airly regular basis. They are not, though, the conventional girls and oys of other writers: usually, they are bizarre characters, either gifted or ursed with strange talents—or just plain screwballs.

"Adam and No Eve" resulted from Bester's irritation at the tired last-nan-and-last-woman-on-earth plot. "They Don't Make Life Like They Jsed To" is a later reaction to the same cliché. It is far lighter in tone and ven less clichéd than "Adam and No Eve"; it is also funny. But, given a hoice, earth might better bet on Krane's lone body than on Linda Jeilson and Jim Mayo, who meet in New York City after an atomic blast although the buildings still stand, and there are no bodies mentioned). erhaps the blast has weakened their minds, as they behave like repubescent children. Bester calls them "kooks" (*STL*). She is most in-erested in decorating her Central Park boathouse while he wants to find television repairman (his television has ceased to work, and he assumes is broken). She collects dolls, and he throws a temper tantrum when he earns she has thrown away some model boats. At one point he agrees vhen she says, ". . .you're a guy and I'm a girl, and we've got nothing to ffer each other." Although the story contains some lovely irony (each f them innocently mentions at least once in the course of the story the ong, lonely nights) and a good deal of humor (Linda fills in the public ibrary register with "Last Man on Earth" in the space for business affiliation), Linda and Jim are just too kooky—or retarded. They final do fall into bed together in a mutual revelation while their toys get swe onto the floor, but they have waited so long that the sudden passic (even, or especially, in the face of imminent destruction by enormous i sects) seems as illogical as the long lack of passion.

A more credible couple, Jake Madigan and Florinda Pot, appears "Something Up There Likes Me," whose background is very close contemporary reality (or rather, that of the 1960's): a space center pr ject to launch a biological experimentation satellite. Jake and Florin may be the most engaging and believable couple in all of science fictio Both are very intelligent, but just a bit wacky. The plot operates on tw levels: the love story of Florinda and Jake (who meet as opponents, ba tling over the project), and their satellite, OBO (Orbiting Biologic Laboratory). When OBO is launched, the story of its growing sentienc and the story of their love fuse. As the narrator (who, we learn muc later, is a computer of some sentience itself) comments,

> There's such an emotional involvement with your first satellite tha you're never the same. A man's first satellite is like his first love a fair. Maybe that's why Madigan grabbed Florinda in front of th whole blockhouse and said, "My God, I love you, Florrie Pot. Maybe that's why she answered, "I love you, too, Jake." Mayb they were just loving their first baby.

From that point on, OBO is their baby, their child, and he sees them his parents (even wanting them to get married so he will not be i legitimate). OBO finally gains control of the whole country through complete interface with every electronic circuit. Jake and Florinda hav become another version of Adam and Eve, but a viable version with strong and healthy child who just might bring salvation to the world a he forces people to act morally and ethically (or at least that is what hi parents are hoping). OBO's godlike powers and his symbolic role ar suggested when Jake tells Florinda that he wants no carrots to eat (a car rot on board OBO had supposedly aided his leap to sentience): "That's little too close to transubstantiation for me." Adam and Eve hav become their parallels in the New Testament, Joseph and Mary, offerin the world a possible savior.

Love also influences the characters in "The Pi Man" and "The Four Hour Fugue." Both have protagonists with strange gifts that becom deadly, and both offer love relationships as solutions to the problems o the protagonists. The Pi man, Peter Marko, is another compulsive, bu on a grand scale. Like the elderly couple in Shirley Jackson's "One Or dinary Day, With Peanuts," Marko is driven to compensate, to balanc the activities around him with his own actions. If restaurant customer are drinking too much cream, he must have black coffee; the rooms i his apartment must be contstructed into a symmetrical pattern, regard less of the expense. His impulses drive him at times to acts of apparentl gratuitous violence:

I respond to the patterns of the entire galaxy, maybe universe; sight and sound, and the unseen and unheard. I'm moved by the patterns of people, individually and demographically; hostility; generosity, selfishness, charity, cruelties and kindnesses, groupings and whole cultures. And I'm compelled to respond and compensate.

He often speaks in a jumble like Solon Aquila's; also like him, Marko is an outsider who seems mad to others and, at times, even to himself. But his compulsion is equaled in strength by Jemmy Thomas' compulsion to love him. That, too, she says, is a pattern she cannot help but follow. Perhaps Jemmy is right, but even if she is not, they agree, "We won't be dogs in the manger. If love's a little thing and has to end, then let it end." As they begin to make love, Marko is able to forget all patterns but this one: "God damn the world. God damn the universe. God damn. GGG-o-dddddddd." Love seems to offer the only hope, the only pattern which subsumes all other patterns.

Blaise Skiaki, protagonist of "The Four-Hour Fugue," is gifted with a supernormal sense of smell (the overpopulated society where water is so scarce that perfume has become a necessity is a brief but fine piece of background extrapolation for the story). Unfortunately, he is also subject to sleepwalking periods when he becomes a different person, Mr. Wish, following the pheromone trails of those who wish to die. The company he works for attempts to solve the mystery of his behavior by hiring experts (much like the bureaucracies of "Disappearing Act" and "Time is the Traitor"). Gretchen Nunn is called in: her gift of "extrasensory perception of other people's senses" is equal to Skiaki's gift. She, too, however, has an almost-fatal weakness and, as she learns of Skiaki's second personality and the two fall in love, he discovers her blindness. The plot is far less interesting, though, than the characters who learn from one another and are stronger at the end than they were before because they are now both aware and together.

But of all Bester's short stories over the years, "Fondly Fahrenheit" remains his most popular and strongest. A dramatic production of it was done for Producer's Showcase in the 1950's, and the Science Fiction Writers of America selected it for inclusion in the *Science Fiction Hall of Fame*. Its depiction of a deranged mind and the interface between the human and the synthetic creation traces its lineage back to Shelley and continues in Phillip K. Dick. One interpretation of *Frankenstein* is that Frankenstein and his creation are halves of the same whole. Jeff Riggenbach, in "Science Fiction as Will and Idea: The World of Alfred Bester," (see secondary bibliography) argues persuasively that "Fondly Fahrenheit" is a Doppelganger story with James Vandaleur the evil side and his android the good side; in the end the evil conquers the good without ever even realizing that he is evil. Bester utilizes the split self in *TDM* and in his non-science fiction novel, *Who He?* (all three works were written within the same three-year period). But, since Bester's concerns are usually less moral than psychological, it may be an oversimplification to speak of Vandaleur and his android in terms of good and evil. Rather, Vandaleur is psychotic, a mass of rage so powerful that he transforms the android into a homicidal maniac. That the two personalities blend, there can be little doubt: the narrative point of view shifts from first person (sometimes singular, sometimes plural) to third-person limited to third-person omniscient. Since the identities of both owner and android blur and fuse, so must the point of view.

Vandaleur's psychosis is clearly suggested right from the beginning. As he flees Paragon III, and on subsequent occasions, he beats the android, even though logic should tell him, as the android itself does, that this will do him no good because androids feel neither pleasure nor pain. Beside beating the android and weeping like a child, he can think of nothing to do but hide. As Riggenbach mentions, Vandaleur rationalizes that he cannot sell his android because he can make money by hiring it out, but he hires it out for menial jobs that cannot pay very much. He does not sell it because it is a part of him, and he of it.

The cause of his mental illness becomes clear in references Vandaleur makes to his father. He tells Dallas Brady that "I'm good for nothing next to specialist androids and robots." Then he damns his wealthy father who supported him all his life but "had to go bust just before he died." The picture emerges of a totally dependent, probably pampered child, aware of his inability to succeed on his own without his father's money, but forced, because of his father's death, to make it on his own. Clearly he cannot, and the anger at his father for placing him in that position has boiled over into psychosis. The android murders the first victims, but it is Vandaleur who wants to kill, to avenge himself on a world that snatched comfort and security from him.

"Fondly Fahrenheit" is also a tightly structured tale with little melodrama and few gratuitous actions. Its structure depends upon a scenic arrangement of material and a densely woven pattern of imagery. The story is told in eight scenes: four major ones, set on different planets where murder is the central action; two intervals where Vandaleur decides where to go next; the escape scene; and the final scene where a new android under Vandaleur's influence is about to commit murder again. Each scene develops action and character and repeats images that unify the entire work. The main image is, of course, heat. In the first three murders, the temperature is high (hot weather, hot furnace in the jewelry workshop, hot furnace in the power plant). The android requires that heat to override its programming and kill, but the heat also adds to the intensity of the scenes. Part of the horror of the murders results from the glee the android seems to feel as it kills (here, we may sense Vandaleur's own relief as a valve is provided for his buried rage)—the repeated choruslike song ("All reet! All reet!") and the repeated dance it does, its fingers "writhing in a strange rumba all their own." The last two murders are committed by Vandaleur and, although he does not need the heat, he does set fire to Blenheim's house, continuing the pattern. Only in the murder of Nan Webb is that image missing.

Bester calls "Fondly Fahrenheit" "a quintessential example of one of my strongest patterns, my heat-death compulsion. . ." (*STL*). And the two are inextricably linked here, not only in the practical necessity of providing the android with conditions under which it can kill, but in the very landscape itself. The opening scene on Paragon III presents a vivid picture of light, fire, and grimness: "a burning sky of orange"; clouds "like smoke"; a "smoking sky"; and a "smoky sunset." Against this moves a line of beaters "like a writhing snake." In the climactic escape scene, all these are repeated, building the story to a fever pitch and tying together the beginning (the android's first murder) and the end (its destruction by fire). Once more there are smoke, a marsh (like the rice paddies on Paragon III), flames, and, again, a line of beaters. The murderer meets its end in a setting parallel to that of its first victim.

As a study of insanity and the split self, "Fondly Fahrenheit" goes unsurpassed. It has become a classic, and deservedly so. Rarely do we have the experience in literature of coming so close to a madman that we share, through the splitting narration and vivid imagery, his nightmares.

The list of Bester's science fiction short stories is not long (it is even startlingly short when compared with those of writers as well known and as highly regarded as he), but the works on it are well worth careful study. The solid craft and inventiveness in character and theme assure many of them permanent places in the science fiction canon.

VII.

ANNOTATED BIBLIOGRAPHY OF SCIENCE FICTION

This listing includes Bester's science-fiction novels and short stories. Since his works are not that numerous, each story is listed separately. Since most originally appeared in magazines, that information is given first. If the story has been reprinted in a collection or anthology, the most easily available source is also given. In the case of title changes, only the currently used title is used for listing. Discussions of most works found in this bibliography can be found in the text of this book (see the index for specific titles).

"Adam and No Eve." *Astounding*, September 1941; *Star Light, Star Bright*, 1976. Stephen Krane destroys Earth with the exhaust from his self-built rocketship but returns to surrender his body to the sea so that life can begin to evolve again.

"The Animal Fair." *Fantasy and Science Fiction*, October 1972. James James Morrison Morrison Weatherby George is raised more by the talking animals in his parents' barn than by his family; the ending suggests that he, when older, intends to lead them in an animal rebellion.

"The Biped, Reegan." *Super Science Stories*, November 1941. The last stages of an ant-human war are narrated by an ant; at the end, a surviving human soldier and the last woman left alive escape on a rocketship.

"The Broken Axiom." *Thrilling Wonder*, April 1939. This is Bester's first published short story. Dr. John Halday uses the matter transmitter he has built and finds himself in a reality with a different atomic structure where he is interrogated by strange beings until being brought back to his lab by his assistant's reversing the machine.

The Computer Connection. New York: Berkley, 1975; London: Eyre Methuen, 1975, as *Extro*. A future Earth, much changed politically and structurally, contains a group of immortals, one of whom becomes linked with a computer bent on world domination through the use of cryonauts, men mutated by cryonics. The novel's narrator, Edward Curzon, and other immortals succeed in foiling this plan. The novel is full of satiric extrapolation from contemporary society.

The Dark Side of the Earth. New York: New American Library, 1964; Toronto: Signet, 1964. A collection of stories, most of them reprinted from magazines: "Time is the Traitor," "The Men Who Murdered Mohammed," "Out of This World," "The Pi Man,"

"The Flowered Thundermug," "Will You Wait?," "They Don't Make Life Like They Used To."

The Demolished Man. Chicago: Shasta Publishers, 1953; London: Sidgwick & Jackson, 1953; New York: Garland, 1975. Ben Reich commits murder in a world where murder has disappeared and many have extrasensory perception. Lincoln Powell, a detective, knows Reich is the murderer, but must discover his motive and his method. Since Reich is psychologically disturbed and self-destructive, Powell must in the end rely on the joined forces of all those with telepathic powers to capture the criminal. This novel won Bester the Hugo Award in 1953.

"The Die-Hard." *Starburst*, 1958. "The Old One" refuses to let his guardians transform him into a cyborg and feels only disgust for this future world he has survived into; at the end he attacks a Galactic Envoy who has the face of a praying mantis.

"Disappearing Act." *New Worlds*, November 1954; *The Light Fantastic*, 1976. The military fight a war for the American Dream; some of the shock victims are able to disappear into their own created pasts, but there is no poet left to explain how fantasies can be made real.

"5,271,009." *Fantasy and Science Fiction*, March 1954; *Starburst*, 1958, as "The Starcomber"; *The Light Fantastic*, 1976. Solon Aquila tries to cure the artist Jeffrey Halsyon of insanity by making him live out his adolescent fantasies.

"The Flowered Thundermug." *The Dark Side of the Earth*, 1964. Sam Bauer and Violet Dugan are shot forward in time from the 1950's to a post-war future reconstructed from the movies.

"Fondly Fahrenheit." *Fantasy and Science Fiction*, August 1954; *The Light Fantastic*, 1976. James Vandaleur tries to learn why his android has become a murderer, while fleeing from the authorities; in fact, he and his android have become psychologically linked and, although the android is destroyed, the killings will continue with Vandaleur's new android.

"The Four-Hour Fugue." *Analog, June 1974; The Light Fantastic*, 1976. Gretchen Nunn discovers that Blaise Skiaki—an expert on scents—sleepwalks, follows people who want to die, and is being used by thugs who murder and loot; at the end, he must rescue her from these thugs.

"Galatea Galante." *Omni*, April 1979. Dominie Manswright, a creator of "biodroids," macrogenerates the "Perfect Popsy" for a client, but the glitch in her programming makes her a succubus: Manswright loves her and intends to court and marry her.

"Guinea Pig, Ph. D." *Startling Stories*, March 1940. Dr. Winter, a psychology professor, learns the lesson of humility after being whisked off to another world where he, like his crayfish, is an experimental animal being "taught" behaviors.

"Hell is Forever." *Unknown Worlds*, August 1942; *The Light Fantastic*, 1976. Five decadents are condemned to live out their fantasies forever by the goddess Astaroth who played a joke on them out of boredom.

"Hobson's Choice." *Fantasy and Science Fiction*, August 1952; *Star Light, Star Bright*, 1976. Addyer, a meek statistician who fantasizes about living in another era, discovers a time machine and is to be sent to another time, but the man in charge of the machine warns him he is suited for no time but his own.

"Life for Sale." *Amazing*, January 1942. A would-be dictator uses a gas that prevents the autonomic breathing response and people must pay for an antidote; the hero and his suffragette girlfriend foil the demonic plot.

The Light Fantastic: The Great Short Fiction of Alfred Bester. New York: Berkley, 1976. This collection of previously published stories includes Bester's comments on each one. "5,271,009," "Ms. Found in a Champagne Bottle," "Fondly Fahrenheit," "The Four-Hour Fugue," "The Men Who Murdered Mohammed," "Disappearing Act," "Hell is Forever."

"The Mad Molecule." *Thrilling Wonder*, January 1941. An eccentric scientist creates a molecule out of hydrogen and electric current that threatens the Solar Universe until a rainstorm destroys it with lightning.

"The Men Who Murdered Mohammed." *Fantasy and Science Fiction*, October 1958; *The Light Fantastic*, 1976. Henry Hassel invents a time machine and tries to change history to prevent his wife's love affair, but he becomes a ghost as a result.

"Ms. Found in a Champagne Bottle." *Status*, 1968; *The Light Fantastic*, 1976. The machines revolt and the narrator, one of the Beautiful People, recounts the rebellion from his cage in the Bronx Zoo.

"No Help Wanted." *Thrilling Wonder*, December 1939. A stranded, penniless Martian applies for a job in the astronomy department of an Earth University but is told he does not know enough about Mars' geography.

"Oddy and Id." *Astounding*, 1950 as "The Devil's Invention"; *Star Light, Star Bright*, 1976. Odysseus Gaul has the gift of luck; although he wishes to use it for the benefit of others, his id directs his talent, and he becomes dictator to adoring slaves.

"Of Time and Third Avenue." *Fantasy and Science Fiction*, October 1951; *Star Light, Star Bright*, 1976. Oliver Wilson Knight finds an almanac from the future; a traveler from the almanac's time convinces him to surrender it.

"Out of This World." *The Dark Side of the Earth*, 1964. The narrator falls in love with a woman from an alternate world where Japan won World War II; because of telephone mix-ups, they meet by phone call.

"The Pet Nebula." *Astonishing Stories*, February 1941. The narrator's roommate makes a tiny nebula that threatens to wreak havoc until it is finally destroyed with a barrage of pure electrons.

"The Pi Man." *Fantasy and Science Fiction*, October 1959; *Star Light, Star Bright*, 1976. Peter Marko is compelled to compensate and balance for all the activities in the universe, but he may be saved by the compulsive love of Jemmy Thomas.

"The Probable Man." *Astounding*, July 1941; *Futures to Infinity*. Ed. Sam Moskowitz. New York: Pyramid Books, 1970. David Conn takes a time machine from 1941 to 2941 where he helps to defeat Nazi descendants, then returns to his own time to fight off the original Nazis.

"The Push of a Finger." *Astounding Stories*, May 1942; *The Astounding-Analog Reader*. Ed. Harry Harrison and Brian Aldiss. Garden City, New York: Doubleday, 1972. When an instrument prognosticates the end of the world in 1000 years, the original cause is traced back to a line of dialogue that can be written as an equation.

"The Roller Coaster." *Fantastic*, June 1953; *Starburst*, 1958. The narrator is a visitor from the passive and dull future whose inhabitants travel back to our time where they amuse themselves by inflicting pain on us.

"Slaves of the Life Ray." *Thrilling Wonder*, February 1941. A madman develops a machine that deforms people horribly; a young intern destroys the madman and his machine.

"Something Up There Likes Me." *Astounding: John W. Campbell Memorial Anthology. New York: Random House, 1973; Star Light, Star Bright*, 1976. Jake Madigan and Florinda Pot become lovers and "parents" to a sentient satellite who controls the world.

Starburst. New York: New American Library, 1958; London: Sphere, 1968. A collection of stories, most of them reprinted from magazines. "Disappearing Act," "Adam and No Eve," "Star Light, Star Bright," "The Roller Coaster," "Oddy and Id," "The Starcomber," "Travel Diary," "Fondly Fahrenheit," "Hobson's Choice," "The Die-Hard," "Of Time and Third Avenue."

Starlight: The Great Short Fiction of Alfred Bester. Garden City, New York: Nelson Doubleday, 1976. This collection of short stories, an essay and an interview combines two shorter collections, *The Light Fantastic* and *Star Light, Star Bright*, published the same year.

"Star Light, Star Bright." *Fantasy and Science Fiction*, July 1953; *Star Light, Star Bright*, 1976. Stuart Buchanan's school principal track down the youngster with the gifted friends and finds himself wished away.

Star Light, Star Bright: The Great Short Fiction of Alfred Bester. New York: Berkley, 1976. This collection of previously published work includes Bester's comments on each piece. "Adam and No Eve," "Time is the Traitor," "Oddy and Id," "Hobson's Choice," "Star Light, Star Bright," "They Don't Make Life Like They Used To," "Of Time and Third Avenue," "Isaac Asimov" (an interview), "The Pi Man," "Something Up There Likes Me," "My Affair with Science Fiction" (essay).

The Stars My Destination. [Rev. Ed.] New York: New American Library, 1957; London: Sidgwick & Jackson, 1956, as *Tiger Tiger!*; Boston: Gregg Press, 1975. Gully Foyle, a brutal man, is bent on revenge after having been shipwrecked in space and ignored by a would-be rescue ship. People in this future society travel by "jaunting" (instantaneous self-teleportation). Gully learns how to be human and discovers that he is capable of space and time jaunting: the less-than-human hero becomes super-human.

"They Don't Make Life Like They Used To." *Fantasy and Science Fiction*, October 1963; *Star Light, Star Bright*, 1976. Linda Neilson and Jim Mayo are the last man and woman on Earth, but each is more interested in childish games than one another until the end when destruction by huge insects is imminent.

"Time is the Traitor." *Fantasy and Science Fiction*, September 1953; *Star Light, Star Bright*, 1976. John Strapp searches for a woman exactly like his dead fiancée, but when his best friend has her cloned, Strapp does not recognize her.

"Travel Diary." *Starburst*, 1958. Diary entries by a bored future socialite who travels from planet to planet show she sees and does nothing she could not do at home.

"The Unseen Blushers." *Astonishing*, June 1942. The narrator meets and believes a stranger at a luncheon for pulp writers who is a time traveler from the future researching a pulp writer considered by the 23rd century as another Shakespeare.

"Voyage to Nowhere." *Thrilling Wonder*, July 1940. Three criminals flee Jupiter to escape extradition to their home planets, but each meets his fate in precisely the way his home planet would have decreed.

"Will You Wait?" *Fantasy and Science Fiction*, March 1959; *The Dark Side of the Earth*, 1964. The narrator tries to sell his soul to the devil but becomes a victim of 20th-century red tape.

VIII.

ANNOTATED BIBLIOGRAPHY
OF BESTER'S COMMENTS ON SCIENCE FICTION

A detailed discussion of Bester's life as a writer and his feelings about science fiction literature can be found in chapter one of this text. This list provides primary sources for the reader interested in Bester as a critic and as a professional writer. The listing includes the most easily available source(s) for each item.

"Alfred Bester." Interview by Darrell Schweitzer. *Amazing*, May 1976; *SF Voices*. Baltimore, Maryland: T-K Graphics, 1976, pp. 6-17.
Bester comments on his writing methods and those of other writers and discusses standards for writing.

"Alfred Bester." Interview by Paul Walker. *Luna Monthly* No. 35/36 (1972); *Speaking of Science Fiction: the Paul Walker Interviews.* New York: Luna Publications, 1978, pp. 302-314.
This repeats much of the content of "My Affair with Science Fiction," but it does offer Bester's definition of "artist" and "hack."

"Books." *Fantasy and Science Fiction*, October 1960-July 1961; September 1961-April 1962; June 1962-July 1962.
Bester was book reviewer for 20 issues. February and March, 1961, are particularly interesting for his angry critique of bad science fiction and a composite picture of his ideal science fiction author (qualities of Heinlein, Sturgeon, Sheckley, Blish, Asimov, Farmer, and Bradbury).

"Epilogue: My Private World of Science Fiction." *The Worlds of Science Fiction*. Ed. Robert P. Mills. New York: Dial Press, 1963, pp. 340-349.
Bester discusses his Commonplace Book, the journal he keeps, and gives sample entries from it.

"Here Come the Clones." *Publishers Weekly*, 14 July 1976; *Algol*, Spring 1977, pp. 35-36.
A short, rather nonsensical science fiction story, filled with clichés, each one footnoted to give a satiric history of science fiction.

"How a Science Fiction Author Works." *SF Symposium*. Rio de Janeiro: Instituto Nacional do Cinema, 1969, pp. 119-128.
In both Portugese and English, this article reprints some remarks made by Bester at a symposium held in Brazil. He talks of the writing of *TDM*, his usual way of constructing a novel, and praises science fiction for being "mind-stretching."

"My Affair with Science Fiction." *Hell's Cartographers: Some Personal*

Histories of Science Fiction Writers. Ed. Brian W. Aldiss and Harry Harrison. New York: Harper and Row, 1975, pp. 46-75; *Starlight*, 1976, pp. 387-409 (in slightly altered form).

Bester speaks primarily of his life as a writer; this is the most important biographical source available.

Responses to a questionnaire, ca. 1963. *The Double: Bill Symposium*. Ed. Bill Mallardi and Bill Bowers. Akron, Ohio: D.B. Press, 1969, pp. 26, 32, 43, 61, 65, 92, 101.

Bester's comments are brief in response to questions dealing with science fiction's relationship to mainstream literature, fandom, the beginning science fiction writer, and the genre's greatest weakness.

"Science Fiction and the Renaissance Man." *The Science Fiction Novel*. Chicago: Advent, 1969, pp. 77-96.

Bester criticizes science fiction for being an unrealistic literature that will appeal only to the reader who is detached from reality and claims a writer is read for his "charm quotient."

"The Trematode: A Critique of Modern S-F." *The Best Science Fiction Stories: 1953*. Ed. Everett F. Bleiler and T. E. Dikty. New York: Frederick Fell, 1953, pp. 11-23.

Bester criticizes science fiction writers for being immature intellectually, emotionally, and technically, but he says he still has hopes for the field.

"Writing and 'The Demolished Man.' " *Algol*, May 1972; *Experiment Perilous: Three Essays on Science Fiction*. New York: Algol, 1976, pp. 29-34.

Bester discusses in some detail the genesis and composition of *TDM*.

IX

ANNOTATED BIBLIOGRAPHY
OF BESTER'S NON-SCIENCE FICTION

Bester has spent his life as a professional writer. His radio and television scripts are both numerous and nearly impossible to locate; a listing of his magazine articles would fill another volume this size. Listed here are only those full-length books and shorter pieces most relevant to him as a writer or to his science fiction.

"Gourmet Dining in Outer Space." *Holiday*, May 1960; *Turning Points: Essays on the Art of Science Fiction.* Ed. Damon Knight. New York: Harper and Row, 1977, pp. 259-266.

A boarding and first meal on a luxury trip to the moon are described. The chef floats in free fall while he prepares gourmet meals on a solar stove; the passengers eat without silverware in free fall. The essay ends with speculation that food garbage dumped in space may result in fields of vegetation thriving in a vacuum 500 years thence.

"Inside TV." *Holiday*, October 1954, pp. 54-61, 79-80, 82-86.

A typical workday at an imaginary television studio is described, with emphasis on the minor incidents that destroy a well-planned show.

"Interview with Robert Heinlein." *Publishers Weekly*, 2 July 1973; *Algol*, November 1973, pp. 32-33.

A rather flippant talk with Heinlein, mostly repetitive of material already covered in other sources. Bester learns he and Heinlein were almost contest competitors with their first stories.

"Isaac Asimov." *Publishers Weekly*, 17 April 1972; *Starlight,* pp. 338-342.

The interview is short and superficial, focusing mostly on Asimov's biography and his science writing.

The Life and Death of a Satellite. Boston: Little, Brown, and Co., 1966.

An explanation for the average reader of the space program, including interviews with numerous experts, explanations of various programs and problems, and terminology, as well as a final chapter on the various responses to the question of whether so much money should be spent on such a program. The book ends with the statement that the space program is "20th-century poetry, an unheard-of poetry of tremendous dimensions. And who questions the cost of a poem?"

Who He? New York: Dial Press, 1953; Berkley, 1956, as *The Rat Race.*

Jordan Lennox writes for a television show that is receiving threatening letters. He tries to locate the writer and discovers that he himself has been writing them when he is drunk. The novel details a sordid behind-the-scenes setting of the television world. It is most interesting for its similarity in plot and character to *TDM*.

"Writing the Radio Mystery." *Writer*, December 1951, pp. 392-395.
This is an explanation to the beginning writer of various methods of structuring a radio mystery (the "closed story" where the murderer is not revealed until the end and the "open mystery" where the audience knows, but the detective does not).

X.

SECONDARY BIBLIOGRAPHY

I. Biographical and Critical

There is no previous book-length study on Alfred Bester. What little is available runs the gamut from brief references to a few full-length essays and book reviews. This first section lists those in the first two categories, followed by a second section listing selected book reviews.

Allen, L. David. *"The Demolished Man."* In *Science Fiction Reader's Guide*. Lincoln, Nebraska: Centennial Press, 1974, pp. 73-83.
This offers primarily a long, detailed plot summary that segments the novel into topics: detective story, psychology, esper society, love story, etc.

"Bester, Alfred." *Contemporary Authors*. 1975 ed.
This provides three paragraphs that outline life and works to the early 1960's. A quotation from Bester suggests his hostility to those who would try to find out about his life.

"Bester, Alfred." *The Science Fiction Encyclopedia*. Ed. Peter Nicholls. Garden City, New York: Dolphin Books, 1979.
A page-long survey of Bester's life and works, this is probably the best complete reference source available, although a few minor mistakes are made.

Bier, Jesse. "The Masterpiece in Science Fiction: Power or Parody?" *Journal of Popular Culture*, 12 (Spring 1979), pp. 604-610.
Science fiction, as exemplified by Bester's *TSMD*, is misanthropic and schizophrenic, resulting in self-parody: "neither he nor the genre as a whole can ever be thought of in terms of true greatness or integrated power."

Delany, Samuel. "About 5,750 Words." In *The Jewel-Hinged Jaw*. New York: Berkley, 1977, pp. 21-36; Elizabethtown, NY: Dragon Press, 1977, pp. 33-49.
Two pages of this essay contain some very cogent and thought-provoking comments on the mysticism found in *TSMD* as well as the novel's use of Rimbaud. Delany calls *TSMD*, "the greatest single s-f novel."

_____. "Introduction" to *The Cosmic Rape* by Theodore Sturgeon. Boston: Gregg Press, 1977, pp. vii-ix.
Delany compares Sturgeon and Bester, commenting on Bester's failure that results from excess, but "almost all of Bester's work achieves a perfection of one kind or another."

Godshalk, William L. "Alfred Bester: Science Fiction or Fantasy?" *Extrapolation*, 16 (May 1975), pp. 149-155.

TDM is "critical fantasy" with the purpose of criticizing science fiction itself through its use of absurdity and parody, particularly in its settings and its psychologically absurd motivations.

Knight, Damon. *In Search of Wonder*. Chicago: Advent, 1967, pp. 234-236.
    Knight criticizes the illogic, inconsistencies, and mistakes of the science in *TSMD*. He calls Bester "the caustic satirist of neurotic science fiction."

"Meet the Author of This Prize Story." *Thrilling Wonder*, April 1939, p. 64.
    An editor's blurb about the young author, stressing the variety of his interests.

Nolan, William F. "Alfred Bester." In *The Human Equation: Four Short Novels of Tomorrow*. Los Angeles: Sherbourne Press, 1971, pp. 1-9.
    An essay based on an interview with Bester, this gives some biographical and critical information. It is nicely put together, although not particularly probing.

Platt, Charles. "Attack-Escape: An Article About Alfred Bester." In *New Worlds Quarterly #4*. Ed. Michael Moorcock. London: Sphere Books, 1972, pp. 211-221.
    A general discussion of Bester's works with biographical commentary and remarks from Bester on his writing methods.

Riggenbach, Jeff. "Science Fiction as Will and Idea: The World of Alfred Bester." *Riverside Quarterly*, 5 (August 1972), pp. 168-177.
    This essay discusses Bester's obsessed heroes who drive the world to social change. Themes are reinforced by imagery of fire and animal brutality, allusions and ironies, all of which point up Bester's "compulsive, violent, world-view." This is probably the best critical essay on Bester available.

Tuck, Donald H[enry]. "Bester, Alfred." *The Encyclopedia of Science Fiction and Fantasy*. Vol. 1. Chicago: Advent, 1974.
    This briefly summarizes significant biographical data and offers a listing of basic titles, dates, and editions of works.

"Who and Where." *Holiday*, October 1954, p. 33.
    This brief biographical sketch introduced Bester to *Holiday* readers.

Williams, Paul. "Introduction" to *The Stars My Destination* by Alfred Bester. Boston: Gregg Press, 1975, pp. v-xv.
    This essay provides some background information on Bester and a brief, but careful analysis of Gully Foyle's transformation.

II. Book Reviews

Boucher, Anthony. "Recommended Reading." *Fantasy and Science Fic-*

tion, August 1958, pp. 106-107.

Starburst is called "one of the most notable single-author collections ever published in our field."

Clute, John. "Books." *Fantasy and Science Fiction*, February 1977, pp. 45-48.

A page is spent in harsh judgment of *TCC*, then *The Light Fantastic* and *Star Light, Star Bright* are reviewed, with the comment that Bester's peak works are "passable excursions into the demonology of the self" and that "their pyrotechnics work as an explanatory dialogue between the inner and the after worlds."

Conan, Neal J. "Alfred Bester, *The Stars My Destination.*" *Science Fiction Review*, March 1975, pp. 18-19.

Conan calls the novel "one of the great romantic adventures," although he thinks the ending bogs down in romanticized social consciousness.

Conklin, Groff. "*Galaxy*'s Five Star Shelf: *The Demolished Man.*" *Galaxy*, September 1953, pp. 121-122.

Conklin calls the novel "psychological surrealism" which takes the neuroses of contemporary city life to their furthest extrapolation.

Delap, Richard. "*The Demolished Man* by Alfred Bester." *Delap's F and SF Review*, October 1975, pp. 8-9.

The novel is still one of the most exciting in the field for its exploration of the human psyche in an extrapolated milieu. Its only weakness is the love story of Barbara and Powell.

_____. "*The Stars My Destination* by Alfred Bester." *Delap's F and SF Review,* November 1975, pp. 8-9.

The novel wields influence, but is flawed because of its preposterous events and Foyle's excessive obsession. However, it is often witty and humorous.

Flood, Leslie. "Book Reviews." *New Worlds*, August 1956, pp. 126-128.

Flood describes *TSMD* as using "literary shock tactics—dramatic sentences, completely amoral characters, lacings of sex, and descriptions of mental torture." The authorial intrusion at the end is "as though Olaf Stapledon had finished a manuscript by Heinlein and Kornbluth and Spillane." The novel is, nevertheless, one of the 10 best science fiction novels of all time.

Jonas, Gerald. "Of Things To Come." *New York Times,* 20 July 1975, p. 10.

TCC suffers from arbitrariness: fantastic premises, eccentric characters, and breathless writing.

Knapp, L. J. "Alfred Bester, *The Light Fantastic.*" *SF Review Monthly*, July-August 1976, pp. 8-9.

Knapp singles out "Hell is Forever" for praise, calling it "uncannily similar to Sartre's *No Exit.*"

Miller, Dan. "Science Fiction." *Booklist*, 1 September 1976, p. 22.
Bester is called "an inspired madman whose freewheeling ideas and stylistic pyrotechnics have long been acclaimed." The stories in *The Light Fantastic* and *Star Light, Star Bright* show "an almost unmatched virtuosity and flamboyance. . . ."

Miller, P. Schuyler. "The Reference Library: *The Demolished Man*." *Astounding,* December 1953, pp. 149-150.
Miller predicts that *TDM* will be a classic: the best combination of mystery and future setting in memory.

_____. "The Reference Library: *The Stars My Destination*." *Astounding*, November 1957, p. 148.
Although its setting is fascinating, the science of *TSMD* "won't hold water—or even molasses." It is not up to *TDM*.

_____. "The Reference Library: *The Dark Side of the Earth*." *Analog*, August 1966, p. 166.
Miller gives the collection a glowing review, calling "The Flowered Thundermug" a wild comedy that parodies a variety of short fiction types.

Paskow, David C. "Reviews." *Luna Monthly*, April 1971, p. 24.
Paskow objects to the violence and typographical devices in *TSMD*.

Patten, Frederick. "*The Computer Connection*." *Delap's F and SF Review*, July 1975, pp. 5-6.
Although the novel is lacking in originality, its characters are believeable and its settings "grotesquely amusing."

Robinson, Spider. "*Galaxy* Bookshelf." *Galaxy*, September 1975, p. 39.
Robinson calls *TSMD* a masterpiece and says, "reading Bester has some of the salient aspects of juggling live chain-saws."

Santesson, Stefan. "Universe in Books." *Fantastic Universe,* August 1957, p. 113.
The writer gives *TSMD* a bad review, asking, is "violence (or rather blind, dogged hate) plus basic English, plus sex and deliberately exaggerated characterizations. . .an admissible substitute for plotting?"

Searles, Baird. "Alfred Bester, *The Computer Connection*." *The SF Review Monthly*, May 1975, pp. 21-22.
TCC is dated and illogical, but still a good read.

Schweitzer, Darrell. "The Vivisector." *SF Review*, August 1977, p. 75.
Bester has always been ahead of everyone else. The stories in *The Light Fantastic* and *Star Light, Star Bright* use "lunatic, brilliant invention" to demolish clichés.

"SF Book Review." *Thrilling Wonder*, August 1953, p. 146.
TDM is clever and dazzling, like "a three-ring circus going on at all times," but it "is neither great nor dismissable as a *tour de force*."

Silverberg, Robert. "Infinity's Choice: *Starburst*." *Infinity*, November 1958, pp. 94-95.

Though "Travel Diary" and "The Die-Hard" are trivial and "The Roller Coaster" incoherent, the other stories are excellent, especially in their deflation of clichés.

_____. "Silverbob's Book Review Corner." *Odyssey, Spring 1976, p. 14.*

TCC lacks the invention and scope of Bester's earlier novels, but it does show the "calculated effects" of a professional. "Bester's third-best novel is superior to almost anyone else's best-best."

_____. "The Spectroscope." *Amazing*, December 1964, pp. 123-124.

The Dark Side of the Earth is an uneven collection from the original "The Pi Man" to the vacuous "Out of This World" and heavy-handed "The Flowered Thundermug."

Stableford, Brian. "*The Light Fantastic* by Alfred Bester." *Vector*, June 1977, pp. 15-16.

Bester's stories are "a reflection of inner landscapes," and Bester is an exceptional, perhaps uniquely independent writer.

Warren, George. "Plugged-In: An Essay-Review." *SF Review*, February 1976, pp. 28-30.

Warren offers a detailed and negative review of *TCC*, calling it a "mistake." Each hint of a traditional plot is sabotaged for "silly verbal fireworks."

INDEX

6737.